A PROMISE FOR TOMORROW

D1684982

British Library Cataloguing in Publication Data available

This Large Print edition published by AudioGO Ltd, Bath, 2012.
Published by arrangement with the Author.

U.K. Hardcover   ISBN   978 1 4713 0428 6
U.K. Softcover   ISBN   978 1 4713 0429 3

Copyright © Miranda Barnes 2012

Printed and bound in Great Britain by
MPG Books Group Limited

A FRESH START

'I think that's everything,' the estate agent said. 'Anything else?'

'No, thank you,' Sarah said. 'You've covered it all very well.'

'If there is anything else, you have my number. Or you can just call in and see us. We're in the main street, Bondgate Within.'

'Thank you again.'

The man smiled and held out his hand. 'Welcome to Alnwick, Miss Hodgkin!'

On her own at last, Sarah took a deep breath and began to explore the flat that was to be her new home.

She had been through it a couple of times, but always in the company of someone from the agency. Now she wanted to experience it for herself. As she thought of it, she wanted to *understand* it, and see how she might fit in.

It was a modern flat in a nice, old building close to the town centre. A Georgian town house, the agency had said. So once it had been a house for a single family, plus all the servants and helpers the family needed to keep them warm, clean and fed.

Now it had been split into half-a-dozen comfortable flats for single people and couples. Marty would have hated it, she thought with a wry smile. His ideal was to live in a new-build on the Quayside. But it suited her very well.

A smart little galley kitchen, bathroom, living-room with dining area and a bedroom. Furnished, too. Everything a single girl like her needed.

There was even provision for tenants to store things in the basement, in little rooms they could lock.

Not that she had much with her to store. All her furniture, and much else as well, had been put into storage back in Newcastle. She really had travelled light. The best way when you needed to make a clean break and get out.

Nothing had changed since her last look round, she decided. The flat was exactly as remembered and signed up for. It was a six-month contract. So that was how long she had to get her life in order.

Perhaps it would be here, or perhaps back in Newcastle. Possibly somewhere entirely different. She didn't know.

It really didn't matter right now. She had made a start. That was the important thing. And here was where she was, starting off afresh.

She jumped as the buzzer on the front door began to make its irritating noise. The estate agent, she thought with an indulgent smile. What had he forgotten to tell her this time?

Last time it had been about spare keys and making electricity readings. He really was a

2

fusspot, a fusspot with a poor memory.

She opened the door, ready to make a joke about memory. But it wasn't the little man who had left only twenty minutes ago. It was a young woman Sarah hadn't seen before.

'Hi! I just thought I would say hello. I live in the flat across the landing,' the woman said, nodding behind her. 'I'm Linda Oliver.'

Sarah smiled. 'Sarah Hodgkin. Come in—please!'

The woman stepped through the doorway. 'I won't stay. I know you've just arrived. I just wanted to say that if you need anything, or want to know where anything is, don't hesitate to give me a shout.'

'Thank you. But the estate agent has covered it all, I think.'

'In incredible detail?'

Sarah laughed. 'Yes, indeed! Microscopic detail. I don't know how he expected me to remember everything he told me.'

'That's him. Mr Wardle. He's all right, though. Just a bit bureaucratic. It's his job, I suppose.'

They moved into the living-room. Linda looked around and said, 'It's very nice, isn't it? I wondered how they had organised this side of the house when they made the flats.'

'It is nice, yes. The decor isn't necessarily what I would have chosen myself but they've obviously had a professional to do it.'

'It's very modern, very fashionable to have

3

these bold colours.'

'Yes, you're right. But my choice would have been a bit more traditional. Paler and less confrontational, perhaps, than purple and cream stripes.'

'Traditional? Oh, yes. My gran would have had flowers everywhere—and flying ducks on the walls!'

'That would have been nice.'

They caught each other's eye and began to laugh. 'It is very nice,' Sarah admitted. 'But I have to have something to complain about.'

'Oh, I know! And there's hardly anything to complain about here, is there? You just have to make the best of it. It's not at all like my last place.'

'Nor mine. You're right. We're very lucky.'

'I'm a local girl, myself. Have you come far, Sarah?'

'Newcastle. I'm a city girl.'

'We could have swapped places if I'd known. I'd love to move there. Not that there's much chance of that happening.'

'Oh, Newcastle has its attractions but I needed a change. Alnwick will be just right for me, I think I used to come here with my parents when I was little, and I always thought it was a lovely old town.'

'It's not bad, I suppose. I hope you're not disappointed.'

'Thank you. I'm sure I won't be.'

Linda glanced at her watch and grimaced.

4

'I'd better be off. I'm on my way to work, and I'm running late.'

'Do you work locally?'

'Yes. I'm a hairdresser. I work in a salon in the centre.'

'That's handy.'

'It is. Anyway, nice meeting you, Sarah. See you later!'

Sarah smiled and showed her to the door. She stood there for a moment, listening to Linda clattering down the staircase, pleased to have met someone already. It was a good start.

*   *   *

Over a cup of coffee, she sat at the kitchen table and thought about what she had to do. Get a job! That was the top priority. Doing something—anything—that paid a wage. Apart from that, she had to make sure the money she had lasted. Six months she would give it. When the lease for the flat came up in six months' time she would have to be back on her feet—or else!

She would do it, she said firmly to herself. One way or another, she would be back on her feet by then, and moving on.

Her mobile played its tune, reminding her she had meant to get it changed. She was sick of hearing 'Greensleeves', or whatever it was.

She glanced at the screen. Marty! She hesitated. Did she really want to talk to him just now? She grimaced and pressed the button.

'Hello, Marty. What can I do for you?'

'Just wondering where you've got to and how you are. That's all.'

'I'm fine thank you. You?'

'Oh, you know. Missing you.'

'It's no good, Marty. I don't want to go through all that again. We made our decision. Let's stick to it.'

'Did we really? Are you sure we made a decision?'

'Yes,' she said firmly. 'We both knew we weren't right for each other. We'd been together long enough to know our own minds, and when you told me you didn't really want to get married and have children I knew it was time to call it a day.'

'We might have had our differences, but . . . well, I didn't mean for us to finish altogether.'

'But I did, Marty. It was good while it lasted. Let's leave it at that. Goodbye, Marty. I hope you find what you're looking for in life.'

'Sarah . . .'

She ended the call. Then she took the back off the phone and removed the SIM card. She would get a new one, and a new number.

A clean break should be just that. She wasn't prepared to have Marty phoning her every five minutes to see if she had changed her mind. There was no future in that.

Already, in fact, she couldn't understand

why she had stayed with him so long. Why on earth hadn't she realised earlier that he wasn't right for her, or she for him?

She dropped the SIM card into the bin. She would keep the phone, though. No need to throw that away, as well. All she needed to do was find a phone shop in town and get a new SIM card. There was bound to be one somewhere.

In fact, she thought, glancing around, she would do that right now. There was no point in being cut off from every part of the outside world.

She had done what she could here for the moment. Her cases and bags were unpacked, and her things put away. She had no reason to delay. She could do some grocery shopping while she was out. Immerse herself properly in local life.

She closed the door behind her and locked it. When she glanced out of the window on the landing she could see her little car in its parking place.

She smiled. It made a change to be going out without needing a car, or a bus or the Metro.

Her feet were going to rediscover their purpose. Small town life was going to be a big adventure, she thought with amusement. And here I come!

A NEW FRIEND

Alnwick was busy. A watery sun gave a hint of spring, and people had responded by coming out in their droves.

One thing about this town, Sarah thought as she edged along the pavement, was that it did have a real centre. Lots of interesting little shops, as well as all the usual banks and estate agents and travel agencies, for people who didn't find Alnwick sufficient.

She liked the historic buildings, too. It looked like a town that had been here a long time, as indeed she knew it had.

She stepped into a newsagents and bought a copy of the local weekly paper, thinking that would be as good a place as any to start job hunting.

When she came back outside an argument had started between a young woman with fiery red hair and a traffic warden. For some inexplicable reason, the woman was objecting to the folded paper the man had tucked under the windscreen wiper of her car.

'Five minutes!' the woman said indignantly. 'I've been here five minutes, and you have the cheek to give me this.'

'You've been here longer than that,' the traffic warden said bluntly.

'You're taking food out of my children's

mouths. You ought to be ashamed of yourself.'

The man almost responded in kind but somehow he managed to retain his temper. He turned and walked away instead.

'I'm going to stand for election and get you made redundant!' the woman shouted after him.

Sarah moved on, amused, thinking how glad she was her car was safely lodged in its ordained parking place. The fines were such a lot of money these days.

Something, she didn't know what, made her glance back after she'd gone a few paces. The woman was standing still, her head down. With horror, Sarah realised she was in tears. She stopped and went back to her.

'Are you all right?'

The woman shook her head.

'Don't be upset,' Sarah said desperately. She placed a tentative hand on the woman's arm.

The woman shivered, seemed to shake herself and then straightened up. She attempted a smile when she looked at Sarah.

'That man!' she said. 'Who do they think they are, these people? So bossy! They're unbearable.'

Sarah chuckled. 'Well, you didn't let him have it all his own way, did you?'

The woman sighed. 'It's just one of those days, I'm afraid. I should have stopped in bed this morning.'

'We all get days like those.'

The woman looked thoughtful for a moment. 'Now I've actually *bought* that parking place, I don't need to worry about getting another ticket, do I?'

'Well . . . I suppose not, no.'

'So the car can stop there all day?'

'Well . . .'

Sarah wasn't sure about that.

'Come on, then! Let me buy you a cup of coffee. You've been very kind.'

'Well . . .' Sarah said again.

'I mean it!' the woman warned. 'Don't you let me down, as well.'

Sarah laughed and nodded acceptance. She was relieved the woman seemed to have recovered her composure.

*   *   *

A little coffee shop nearby, in the basement of an old town house, gave them the refuge they sought. They ordered a skinny latte and a cappuccino. No cakes or cookies, Sara was relieved to see. Life was a struggle enough. She didn't need more temptation.

'I'm India,' the woman with fiery red hair said.

'Oh?' She tried not to smile. 'And I'm Sarah.'

'What's more, I'm totally, absolutely depressed and despondent. Far worse than I was yesterday. I need someone's ear to pour all my misery into, and you're the lucky one.'

Sarah chuckled. 'I could see you were a bit upset back there.'

'A bit! You've no idea. Sixty pounds, that stupid, arrogant man's cost me! Today, of all days. Anyway, it can't get worse. How about you? How's your day going?'

'Wonderfully well, thank you. I've just arrived here and moved into a new flat.'

'Oh? Congratulations.' India beamed and added, 'You're new to Alnwick?'

'Yes. This is my first day. I've visited before, but I'm here to stay now.'

'Well, I hope you like it. I'm sure you will.'

'It seems lovely.'

India nodded. 'It's not a bad little town. Is there just you?'

'Yes. I'm a single girl still.'

'Lucky you!'

Sarah smiled. 'I take it you're not?'

'No. Married, with two children—thirteen and fourteen. They run me ragged—all of them!'

A woman passing their table called a greeting to India and gave Sarah a smile. India responded with something about a music event at the Playhouse.

Sarah half-listened, enjoying the feeling of entering a new world with new people. It was exciting. And she rather liked the strange woman she had just met.

'Have you got a job here?' India asked,

turning back to her.

'No, not yet. But I must start looking?'

'Oh? I assumed you'd come to start a new job.'

'No. This a fresh start for me. New home, new job—I hope!'

'Good luck with that. It's not an easy time for job-hunting. My husband, Harry, just found out this morning that he's being made redundant. That was the last thing we needed.'

'Oh, I'm so sorry! That's awful.'

Sarah guessed that had had something to do with the upset over the parking ticket. One thing after another, it sounded like.

India nodded and looked grim-faced. 'It is,' she said. 'Absolutely dreadful. I must find out where the workhouse is. We're going to need it.'

Sarah was startled. Then she smiled tentatively. 'I don't think they have them any more, do they?'

'No? That's a pity. So where do the hopeless and bereft go these days?'

Sarah was relieved when India touched her wrist lightly with her finger tips and added, 'Just joking. It's not that bad—yet.'

Sarah smiled. 'I must say, you're dealing with adversity very well, India. I don't think I'd be joking, in your position. What a day you're having!'

'Into every life a little rain must fall.'

'I've heard that one before somewhere,'

Sarah said, laughing. 'I don't like it, but it's true, isn't it?'

'Absolutely. It was on an old calendar that used to hang on my bedroom wall when I was little. An early lesson in life's hard knocks.'

Still smiling, Sarah shook her head and asked, 'Where does your husband work?'

'A furniture factory on the industrial estate. It seems that the recession has made its way to Alnwick. The whole place is closing down. Everyone's been given their notice.'

Sarah was quiet for a moment. The news wasn't what she had expected, or wanted, to hear. It seemed to overshadow her own prospects.

'Has Harry been there long?'

'Fifteen years. Since before I met him.' India sighed and added, 'It seems people don't want new furniture any more. What's wrong with them? How can they bear to put up with their old stuff any longer?'

Sarah chuckled. 'They'll come round. I'm sure they will. But the company can't wait, presumably?'

India shook her head. 'They say they're bust. It's been on the cards for a while, and now it's happened.'

Sarah stirred her coffee thoughtfully. She wondered what it must be like to have news like that dropped on you. Terrible. Poor India. No wonder she made jokes of everything. It would be either that or sit in a heap and cry.

13

'Will you be able to manage financially?'

India shrugged. 'I haven't a clue at the moment. Harry's getting his last wages at the end of the week. After that . . .' She shrugged again. 'The benefits office, I suppose, or whatever they call it these days. Job Seekers' Allowance, isn't it?'

Sarah nodded. 'Yes. There's other things, as well. Various benefits, especially for people with families. But I'm not familiar with them. You can even defer mortgage payments, I think. Help like that.'

'I'll have to get busy,' India said with a frown. 'Lots of people to talk to, I suppose, and forms to fill in.'

Bound to be, Sarah thought. But so what? Plenty of people were going to be in the same position the way things were going. It was indeed a worrying time. Plenty of people were there already, probably.

Time to change the subject.

'What are your children called?'

'Helen and Mark.'

'Oh? Such lovely classic names.'

'What did you expect? That I'd have children with names as ridiculous as mine? In that case, one would have had to be called Longhoughton and the other Seahouses.'

Sarah stared, puzzled.

'I was born on the hippy trail to Shangri La, or wherever,' India said airily. 'My parents have no sense at all, even though they are

14

Scottish.'

Sarah chuckled. 'Do you have brothers or sisters?'

'A sister. Don't ask—Skye! But it could have been worse.'

'Oh?'

'Just imagine if my parents had been holidaying on the Isle of Muck.'

Sarah began laughing. She didn't stop until they were outside the café and saying their goodbyes. 'We should meet again,' India said. 'Get to know each other properly.'

'That would be nice.'

India scribbled something on a bit of card. 'Here's my phone number. If you need anything, or want to chat, give me a ring. But I'll probably see you again in town anyway.'

'I hope so.'

'And good luck with the job-hunting!'

'Thank you. The same for your Harry. And I hope you manage to wriggle out of your parking ticket.'

'Oh, that old thing! I've forgotten about it already'

Sarah smiled. It was a long time, she thought, since she had met anyone as entertaining as India. She hoped they did meet again.

GETTING NOWHERE

Grocery shopping! Sarah reminded herself with a start. There was nothing at all in the way of food in the flat. Yet somehow food had sunk to the bottom of her to-do list. It wasn't really surprising, she thought with a wry smile. Meeting India had seen to that.

She didn't need much. Just enough to get her started and see her through the day. Coffee, tea and something to eat in the evening.

Cleaning materials, as well. It wasn't a lot, but it still managed to fill three plastic bags. And that made it a struggle to find her key and let herself through the main door and back into the flats.

'Let me help,' a voice said from behind her, as she tried to hold all the bags in one hand and search for her keys with the other.

She turned to see a tall young man waiting patiently.

'I'm sorry!' she said. 'I didn't realise I was holding you up. My key is here somewhere.'

'That's all right. Here!'

He stepped forward and put a key of his own in the lock. Then he opened the door and held it open for her.

'You must be the new tenant?' he said. 'Number three?'

'Yes, that's right. I just arrived this morning. You live here, as well, do you?'

'Yes. Number one. John Stevens is the name.'

'Sarah Hodgkin. I'm pleased to meet you.'

'Let me take some of your bags,' he offered. 'These stairs are brutes when you're fully laden.'

She smiled and accepted the offer gratefully. 'They're good exercise, though,' she said. 'I won't need to join a gym.'

'No. Just going up and down the stairs half-a-dozen times a day is enough for anyone. When you've settled in I'll get you to sign the petition.'

'Oh?'

'For a lift. We're all going to pressure the landlord to put one in even if it has to be built outside, on a wall. One of those high-speed, glass jobs they have in Dubai.'

'Dubai? I've never been there.'

'Neither have I. But I've seen the photos in the glossy mags.'

She laughed. Then they reached her landing and she turned to thank him for his help.

'Any time!' he assured her, before bounding back down the stairs.

What a nice man, she thought happily. It looks as though I'm really lucky with my neighbours. That's two I've met.

*   *   *

She took her time over the next couple of days, easing her way gently into her new life. There was no need to rush.

She didn't want to find herself overwhelmed by difficulties and uncertainty. She would do what had to be done patiently and systematically—and enjoy herself while she did it.

The need to find a job was most pressing but she knew she had to be realistic. It wouldn't be easy. And it wasn't.

She saw nothing in the local paper or in the adverts in shop windows. Nothing for her, and not much for anyone else either.

The next step would be to visit the job centre, but she wasn't quite ready for that yet. It could wait a little longer, wait until she had found her feet in this new life.

Part of her reluctance to take that step immediately was that she wasn't even sure what she wanted to do, or even what she could do here.

She had been such a long time in her old job that she needed time to review her options carefully, and start thinking about what opportunities a small town like Alnwick might have to offer.

There was also a little pride at stake. Never before had she needed to seek help when it came to finding a job. Job centres had always been for other people, not for the likes of her.

So she wanted to see if she could do it herself first, before she went looking for help.

But it wasn't easy. After a week or two of circling round and round, getting nowhere, she began to miss her old job. A new start was proving more difficult to make than she had anticipated.

The old place had been very good for her. She went to the office every morning, sometimes without enthusiasm, it was true, but always knowing she was going to be very busy when she got there. And knowing, too, that what she did when she got there was appreciated.

In fact, she thought with a wry smile, they had probably always been so kind to her on the rare occasions she was ill because they had been desperate to get her back to work as soon as possible.

Perhaps she had made a mistake in leaving? Oh, no! She mustn't think that. Of course she hadn't. There was more to life than work, and she had needed to sort the rest of it out desperately.

It was just that she missed the safe, reliable rhythm of her old job. She had been at Jackson's a long time, after all. Perhaps too long. But she wasn't made for doing nothing, which was what she was doing right now.

She shook her head. Enough! That's it. This very morning, she would swallow her pride and see what the Alnwick job centre had to offer.

Not much. The job centre was a massive disappointment.

'We don't have much on the stocks at the moment,' the woman Sarah dealt with said. 'Not that are suitable for you, I mean.'

'I understand,' Sarah said.

'In fact, we don't have many vacancies suitable for anyone,' the woman confided in a weary voice. 'The recession, you know?'

'Yes, I have heard of it.'

'I'm only temporary myself.'

'Really?'

The woman grimaced.

'Well,' Sarah said, feeling less unusual and isolated, 'I see you have a vacancy for a dog trainer. I could do that—with training, of course. Is it sheepdogs or greyhounds?'

'I'm not sure.'

'Or apprentice blacksmith. That's shoeing horses, isn't it?'

'What does it say?'

The woman leant forward to peer at the screen. 'Shoeing horses,' Sarah said firmly. 'Do you think I could cope with that?'

'As much as anybody, probably,' the woman said with a grin.

'That's what I thought. But I'll give it a miss, I think.' She paged on and reached the end. 'That's everything, isn't it?'

'I'm afraid so. Come back next week. We might have some more vacancies by then.'

'Do you think so?'

20

'Not really. But you never know, do you? Meanwhile, you should fill in the Job Seekers' Allowance application form. That will give you a bit of money. Not much, but it's better than nothing?'

Sarah was glad to get out of there. The experience had been every bit as stultifying and deadly as she had always imagined it would be.

Still, you had to start somewhere if you were looking to resurrect your career, or start a new one.

What she needed now, though, was to see a friendly face, and one had just come to mind.

She hunted through her pockets for the bit of card. Then she rang India to see if she could meet her for coffee.

A PLAN EMERGES

They met outside *Chez Marie,* the café they had I visited the first time they met. Sarah was very pleased to see India's smiling face. 'I'm so happy you could make it,' she said.

'I'm always ready to get out of the house, especially if there's cappuccino to come. How are you, anyway? How are you finding Alnwick?'

'Alnwick is fine, very nice. To be honest, though, I'm a bit flat this morning. I've just come from the job centre.'

'Spotted any opportunities in the job market?'

Sarah shook her head.

'Not really. Just blacksmithing and dog training, which aren't really me.'

India laughed and linked arms with her.

'Come on!' she said. 'I'm buying.'

'No, no! It's my turn.'

'I'm job hunting, too,' India said.

Sarah sipped her coffee. 'What kind of job?'

'Anything. I don't care.'

India shrugged and gave a little sigh. 'We've got to have some money coming into the house. Harry is doing his best, but he hasn't found anything yet. So I'm going to have a go myself.'

'Well, good luck. You'll have to let me know how you get on. What are you qualified for?'

Again the shrug. 'Nothing at all. I'm not qualified for anything useful or practical. So I'll have to see what comes up.'

'But what did you used to do? You must have had a job sometime in your life, India.'

'Me?' India gave a brittle little laugh. 'Nothing much. Shop work mostly, so long as it was nothing to do with arts and crafts.'

'What's wrong with arts and crafts? What's that got to do with anything?'

'My parents.'

Sarah sighed. 'Am I being really silly? What about your parents?'

India grimaced. 'This coffee is terrible. It must be the worst cup of coffee I've ever had in my life. Who made it?'

Sarah nodded towards a girl clearing a table.

'Oh dear! The new girl. I'd better not say anything, in that case. I don't want to get anybody into trouble. What were you saying?'

'I asked you what your parents had to do with it.'

'Oh, yes.' India gathered herself. 'Well, from what I've already told you about where they went and where they lived, what does that tell you about them?'

Sarah shrugged.

'Next to nothing. Oh, wait a minute! Are they crafts people?'

'Heart and soul. A life of great aspiration and poverty. I swore I would do anything but follow in their footsteps.' India shuddered and added, 'And they're still at it!'

Sarah laughed. 'At what? What do they do?'

'Potting. They're potters, Dad more than Mum. She's also into textiles.'

'And do they still live on Skye?'

'Absolutely.' India shuddered again. 'And I hope they stay there.'

'Oh, India! You really are terrible.'

'I swore I would do anything but live like them, and guess what? Here I am with an unemployed husband, no way of keeping up the mortgage payments on the house, looking for a job myself . . . and knowing that all I'm good for is potting!'

'You, too? But I thought . . .'

'That was after they'd taught and trained me. As soon as I reached an age where I could say no, I did.' Sarah smiled. 'So it's not a laughing matter, is it?'

'No, definitely not.'

They looked each other in the eye and somehow ended up in near gales of laughter.

'So perhaps you've got something in mind?' Sarah said eventually, wiping tears from her eyes and trying to suppress more convulsive laughter.

'Well . . . if all else fails, if I really can't get a job, I've begun to think of opening a craft shop. I wouldn't set up a potter's wheel, but I know enough about the craft to buy decent stuff in.'

'I'm sure you do,' Sarah said thoughtfully. 'But it would still take a big investment to get it up and running, and then there would be no certainty of selling enough to make a living, would there? I mean . . . I don't want to be hyper critical, but have you thought it all through?'

'No,' India admitted. 'Not at all. But you're giving me lots of reasons not to think any more about it at all. Maybe I should start an employment agency instead?'

'Now you're talking! You'd be able to help me then, and probably Harry, as well.'

'Mmm. That would be good. So what did you used to do, Sarah? Before you came to Alnwick?'

'I worked in an office.'

'An office?'

'It's no good pulling a face, India,' Sarah said, laughing. 'Yes, an office! And I liked my job, too.'

'What did you do, besides make the tea?'

Sarah chuckled. 'You're wicked! You really are. But you do make me laugh.'

'You can pay, after all, in that case,' India said, pushing back her chair.

On the way out, they bumped into a man India knew. He was buying bread from the shop counter at the front.

'Robert! How are you?' India grabbed hold of his arm.

The man spun round and laughed when he saw who it was. 'I'm fine, thank you, India. And you?'

India grimaced. 'Struggling. Harry's lost his job, and so far hasn't been able to find another one.'

'He will. Don't you worry about that. People like him can do useful, practical things—not like us bureaucrats.'

'This is my friend, Sarah,' India added, drawing Sarah forward. 'She's new to Alnwick.'

Robert smiled and held out his hand.

'Hello, Sarah! You should know you've found bad company already. This woman . . .'

He stopped and grinned. 'I'll say no more. Just that I hope you like it here.'

'Thank you,' Sarah said, smiling back. 'I'm sure I will. I do already, in fact.'

'Good.'

Robert turned to pay for his bread.

'See you!' India called, leading Sarah towards the door.

'Bye!'

'He's a really nice man,' India confided when they were outside. 'A good friend, too. With problems, of course. Terrible problems. All good men come with problems, don't they?'

Sarah wasn't sure about that. In any case, it was hard to believe that a man with such a nice, happy smile as Robert could have too many problems.

ALL ABOUT JOHN

Linda and John Stevens were laughing together at the entrance to the flats when Sarah returned home.

'Hello, you two!' she said, smiling. 'Having fun?'

'Sarah!' John exclaimed. 'Just the person we wanted to see.'

'Oh, yes?'

'We think we should have a party, to

welcome you to Aidan House.'

'Yes,' Linda confirmed. 'It's ages since we had a party here.'

'Well . .' Sarah wasn't sure how she was expected to react. 'It's a nice thought. But I . .'

'In my place,' John added, 'seeing that I've got the biggest flat.'

'Oh? I assumed they were all the same size.' Linda rolled her eyes. 'It makes him feel important, but it just means he pays more rent.'

'Go on—hurt my feelings!' John urged.

Sarah laughed. 'Well, it's very kind of you. But I don't know when . . .'

'Saturday,' John announced. 'I must be off now. You tell her the arrangements, Linda.'

Then he was off, running.

'Goodness!' Sarah said. 'Look at him.'

Linda laughed. 'You'll get used to John. He's a little bit crazy.'

'Fun, though?'

'Oh, yes. Lots of fun. It's hard to take him seriously at times, but he means it about the party. You up for it?'

'I think so,' Sarah said hesitantly.

'You'll have to check your diary?'

'Yes, that's right! No, of course not. It sounds a lovely idea.'

'Do you fancy a coffee? Right now, I mean?'

'Oh yes, please. I'm fed up of job-hunting.'

'Is that what you've been doing?'

'On and off.'

Linda grimaced. 'I know what that's like. Come on! I'll make you a latte.'

'Oh? Impressive.'

'Not really. Wait till you've tasted it. Mum gave me this coffee machine for my birthday, and I'm still practising with it.'

*   *   *

Linda's flat was much the same as Sarah's, except for the wallpaper.

'You have terracotta stripes, I see,' Sarah said as she looked around the living-room. 'I like them better than my purple ones.'

'Not bad, is it? I also have a good view of the street. I like that, being able to see all the movement and activity.'

'I can see trees from my window,' Sarah said. 'That's a big improvement on my place in Newcastle.'

'Onwards and upwards, eh? Now how does this machine work?'

But Linda protested too much. She soon had her new machine hissing and grumbling, and in a few minutes it produced their coffee.

'How's the job hunt going—really?' Linda asked.

'Terrible! Change the subject.'

Linda laughed. 'So what else have you been doing? Anything interesting?'

'Not really. Looking around mostly. But it's early days yet.'

'Of course it is. That's what John used to say before he found his job.'

'John Stevens?'

Linda nodded.

'What does he do?'

'A land surveyor, I think. Something like that. He doesn't talk much about his work.'

'He seems a nice man.'

'Oh, he's lovely!'

'Are you and he . . .?'

Linda laughed. 'If only! No, not really. We've been out for a meal a couple of times, but that's as far as it's gone.'

To her surprise, Sarah felt strangely relieved. She was glad John Stevens wasn't spoken for. Not that she had any interest, of course. How could she? Still . . .

'What are you smiling at?' Linda demanded.

'I was just wondering how many eligible young men there are in this town.'

'Not many,' Linda said. 'And anyway I saw him first!'

Sarah laughed. 'I'm jobless, Linda. Nothing to worry about from me. I'm no competition. All my energies go into hunting for work, not potential husbands.'

But it wasn't completely true. She couldn't spend all her time job-hunting. It was too depressing. John's party sounded like welcome relief.

'I'LL TELL YOU MY NEWS'

The flat soon felt like home for Sarah. Perhaps it wasn't exactly ideal, though. The living-room looked out on to a churchyard rather than the hills or the sea, but at least she could see trees.

The kitchen was rather dark, too, apart from very early in the morning when the sun lit up the breakfast table so brilliantly that she began to wonder about fitting a blind to the window.

She didn't like the colour of the bedroom walls either. And she would rather have had a separate shower cubicle in the bathroom than a shower over the bath. A garden, too.

She would have liked somewhere to plant spring bulbs and potatoes, and lettuce and dahlias. Do all those things she had never done.

But it was home, she thought with satisfaction—her home. The bits and pieces she had added, and the way she had rearranged the furniture meant that it was hers.

It was where she lived now, and she liked it. Just as soon as she found a job, and stopped her money haemorrhaging away, it would be perfect. Well, not perfect, perhaps, but . . . but still wonderful.

She looked up suddenly, startled by the

sound of the front door buzzer. It was a noise she was still getting used to.

'It's me—India!' a weirdly distorted voice said through the entry box.

'Oh, come in, India! There. I've pressed the button to open the door for you. I'm on the second floor.'

She paused and smiled. India! How nice it would be to see her again. She opened the door to the flat and listened to her friend mounting the stairs.

'Nearly there now!' she called encouragingly.

Then she laughed as India came round the final bend on the staircase and sagged helplessly against the wall.

'How on earth . . .' India gasped. 'I've stopped smoking as well.'

Still laughing, Sarah said, 'You get used to the climb. Come on in! How nice to see you,' she added. 'What a lovely surprise.'

'Are you extremely busy?'

'Me? You're joking. Not at all busy. It's wonderful to have a visitor.'

'Sure? You're not filling in job applications or anything like that?'

'Of course not!' Sarah said, laughing again. 'I haven't seen any jobs to apply for.'

She ushered India into the living-room.

'Oh, this is nice! What a lovely flat, Sarah.'

'It's not bad, is it? Let me show you the rest of it.' The tour took all of a minute and a half.

'It's perfect for me.'

'Of course it is. You did well finding it. What a lovely view from the window.'

'Yes. It's a big improvement on my Newcastle flat. I couldn't see any greenery at all from my window there. Coffee?'

'Yes, please! Then I'll tell you my news.'

'Oh? That sounds interesting. Can we make do with instant, by the way?'

'Of course.' India followed her into the kitchen. 'I was going to phone you. Then I couldn't find the bit of paper with your number on. So I thought I'd just try and find you in person.'

'I'm very glad you did. I was getting bored with my own company.'

'You'll never guess what?' India said as soon as they sat down in the living-room with their coffees.

'You've found a job?'

'No! Of course I haven't.' India grimaced. 'But I have got an idea.'

'Oh? Tell me.'

'Well, you know I said the one thing I would never do was have anything to do with arty-crafty things?'

'I remember.'

'So what am I going to do?'

Sarah shrugged.

'Open that craft shop I talked about.'

'You're joking?'

India shook her head. 'I've decided. If

there's one thing I do know anything about, it's arts and crafts. Pots and pictures, and stuff. Textiles, as well.'

Sarah smiled. 'After all you've said about your poor parents!'

'I know, I know. But you've got to be practical, haven't you? And Harry hasn't found a job yet.'

'You are serious, then?'

'Never more so. I thought it through this morning over breakfast.'

Sarah laughed. 'Oh, India! What are you like? You've spent a whole five minutes thinking up this great plan?'

'Longer, actually. I had to wait for the porridge to cool before I could eat it. Anyway, on the way to school with Mark I enquired about a shop that's been empty for months.'

'Really? India, I've not known you long, but it feels like forever . . . in a good way! Anyway, what did they say about the shop?'

India continued. 'They told me the rent, which seems reasonable, and they said I could have it for a craft shop. So it's a go-er. All I have to do now is bring in some stock—and find some customers.'

'There might be a bit more to it than that.'

'True. I'll have to get the electric switched on.'

Sarah started laughing again. India was simply irrepressible. She knew her friend was serious about this, and she wished her well, too. But she had some doubts.

Her own experience of retailing, as well as common sense, told her that a project like this needed more thought than India had apparently given it. Still, you had to admire her energy and enthusiasm.

'What about you?' India asked. 'Have you spotted anything?'

Sarah shook her head. 'Nothing.'

'Oh, I know,' India said. 'It's hopeless, isn't it? That's why I decided to do something myself. But you'll find something. I'm sure you will.'

Sarah wasn't so certain. She wasn't sure there was anything to be found.

'I sometimes wonder if I've done the right thing,' she admitted.

'Moving to Alnwick?'

She nodded.

'Why did you move? You've never told me.'

So she told India about Marty, and how their relationship had ended up going nowhere.

'I was just someone to go to the pictures with, or to a restaurant on rare occasions. I made up the numbers when we went out with friends.' She shrugged and added, 'I was someone for Marty to talk to, and tell what he thought about things. He's a great talker, Marty.'

'And you wanted more than that?'

'I did. Not a ridiculous lot more. I just

34

wanted a normal married, family life. But that was a step too far for Marty. He wasn't ready to leave his youth behind. I'm not sure he ever will be. So it wasn't fun any more. There was nothing much to look forward to, or to plan for. You know?'

India nodded. 'I do. Everyone needs a reason to get up in the morning, even if it's just to earn the money to pay the mortgage.'

'And to dress the children, and make sure they get to school on time?'

India smiled. 'That, too.'

'And to be with the man of your dreams?' Sarah added lightly.

'Harry? Oh, now you're not being serious! Harry doesn't even have a big yacht, never mind a mansion in the country. And he almost never buys me big diamond rings.'

'Stop it!' Sara said, laughing.

'I tell you what,' India added. 'Come and meet him. I was going to ask you, anyway. Can you come for supper with us on, say, Friday? You can make your own mind up then about Harry.'

'I'd love to, India. That would be wonderful. Thank you.'

A PLEASANT EVENING

On the Friday Sarah gave herself a day off from job hunting. She became a visitor again, a tourist, and visited Alnwick Garden, adjacent to Alnwick Castle.

She gathered that the Garden had started off as a project to rehabilitate an abandoned eighteenth-century Italianate garden, and had since become a popular visitor attraction.

What with exhibitions, activity groups of various sorts and different places to eat, plants didn't seem to be the main point of the garden any more.

There were plants still, it was true, and plenty of them, but it certainly wasn't a botanical garden. With its giant tree-house, bamboo maze, complex of water fountains, and souvenir shops, it was more of a place for families to take their youngsters and their elderly relatives on a sunny day.

On that particular day, it wasn't crowded. Sarah sat in the spring sunshine on the terrace outside the main café and idly watched the fountain's jets reach for the sky.

It was lovely, with trees coming into leaf, bamboo quivering in a slight breeze and birds singing all around.

She watched a sparrow pecking around her feet, searching for the crumbs of chocolate cake and bits of flapjack that the previous occupants of her table had left behind. It felt like being on holiday.

Except she was alone. No Marty, or anyone else either. There were times when her new life was very lonely.

Such a long holiday, too, she thought ruefully. Already it was a month since she had left work and arrived in Alnwick. She could scarcely believe it.

She wondered how Marty was getting on without her. With a wry smile, she wondered if he had even noticed she had gone.

If he had, it wouldn't make much difference to his life. Marty was capable of moving on much more easily than she was.

Her thoughts turned to the evening. She was curious. It was hard to imagine how someone like India could have a sensible domestic life.

She smiled. What a little whirlwind she was! Harry would have to be just the same to keep up with her. The children, too. She bet their home life was absolutely frenetic. It would have to be.

*   *   *

India's house was in a modern estate quite close to Alnwick Garden. It was a detached house with a small garden at the front. With bay windows downstairs and dormer windows in a red pantiled roof, it was a very attractive house. Sarah was impressed.

Tentatively, wondering what Harry would be like, she rang the doorbell.

'Come in, come in!' India greeted her. 'You're just in time.'

'Am I late?' Sarah asked anxiously.

'No, no! It's just that you can meet the kids before they go out. Mark is going to football practice and Helen's got a sleep-over at one of her friend's houses this evening.'

India led Sarah into a very cluttered living-room and made the introductions.

'This is my friend, Sarah, everybody. Sarah, this is my son, Mark, and the big one over there is Harry. I don't know where Helen is at the moment. Excuse me please, everybody! I've got something on the hob.'

'Hi, Sarah!' Harry said, coming across to shake her hand.

'Pleased to meet you!' Mark called as he made for the. door. 'Sorry. Can't stop. See you later, maybe.'

Sarah gave him a wave. He was a nice looking boy. Very blond hair and blue eyes. Not many of India's genes evident.

Harry ushered her to a chair. 'Sorry about the mess. But when we're all at home this is what happens. How are you?'

'I'm fine, thank you,' Sarah said, smiling.

It was easy to tell who Mark took after. Harry was just an older version. He was very welcoming and pleasant, too.

'My dear wife tells me you're new to Alnwick?'

'Yes, I am—relatively. But I've been here a month or so, now.'

'Oh, well. You've seen it all then. Everything the old place has to offer. You can't have missed much if you've been here that long.'

'I don't know about that, but I do like what I've seen. Have you lived here long yourself?'

'All my life.' He shrugged and smiled. 'India says you're job-hunting, like me.'

'Yes, indeed. Not very hard, though, and not very successfully. I've seen nothing yet that I could even apply for.'

'Join the club. You have my sympathy.'

India came bustling through the doorway just then.

'Sympathy for what?' she demanded.

'The workers,' Harry told her. 'The workers without jobs.'

'Ah! Now I understand.' She paused and peered at a clock that appeared to have stopped. 'What time is it?'

'Six-thirty,' Harry told her. 'Don't worry. He won't be late.'

'He'd better not be!'

India turned and disappeared again.

'Another friend is coming,' Harry explained.

He might have said more, but just then the door swung open violently and a girl with long, dark hair bounded into the room.

'Anybody seen my laptop?' she demanded. Then, seeing Sarah, 'Oh, hello!'

'You must be Helen,' Sarah said. 'I'm . . .'

'Yes, I know. Sarah. Mum said you were coming.' She smiled and added, 'It's really lovely to meet you.'

'That's very kind of you. And you're off out, too, are you?'

'Yes. I'm just waiting for my lift. My friend's dad . . . oh, that will be him,' she said, hearing the front door bell. 'Excuse me!'

Sarah caught Harry's eye and laughed.

'Kids, eh?' he said ruefully.

'Never a dull moment?'

'Not many, no.'

But it wasn't Helen's lift at the door. As Helen ushered in the new arrival, Sarah saw that it was Robert, the man India had once introduced her to in the café.

'Hello again,' he said, giving her a smile. 'Now then, Harry,' he added. 'Am I late?'

'Not at all,' India called, bustling back into the room. 'A drink anyone? We've just got time.'

*   *   *

Sarah enjoyed the meal and the evening, very much. So did everyone else, it seemed. India had prepared a lamb casserole that she said was from a Moroccan recipe that she used all the time.

That started them all off on a discussion of places, usually countries, they had never visited. It was a long list.

Harry said, 'I used to go south of the Tyne quite often, but I never go down there now. It's too busy.'

'South of the Tyne?' Robert said. 'That's where Gateshead is, isn't it?'

'And London,' Sarah contributed.

'Oh? Is it really?' Robert looked at her. 'You'll have been there, have you? I gather it's not far from Newcastle?'

'Not far, no. And after that you get to France.' Robert nodded and grinned.

'Then Morocco?' India suggested with a rollicking laugh.

'You travellers!' Harry said. 'I can't keep up with you.'

There were more sombre passages to the evening, too. Robert asked Harry if he was having any luck with his job search.

'Not really, no. But something will turn up one of these days.'

'I hope so,' Robert said quietly. He sighed and added, 'It looks as though I might be joining you in the job queue.'

'How do you mean?'

'Redundancy. It's all the rage, isn't it? Everywhere. They let another six go today. By the time everything calms down it will be interesting to see who's left in the old place.'

'Where do you work, Robert?' Sarah asked.

'County Hall. The audit section in accounts.'

'They'll always need accountants,' India said confidently 'You needn't worry.'

'But not as many,' Robert countered. 'They can't afford them.'

'I didn't think they got rid of people in the public sector,' Harry said.

'Temporary staff, mostly. So far. That's what happens these days. They take on people as temporary staff, so they can get rid of them more easily if they have to cut the numbers. I felt sorry for the ones that heard today,' he added.

'We'll all have to come and work in your new shop, India,' Sarah suggested to lighten the mood.

Robert straightened up. 'Tell me more,' he said, giving India her cue.

He seemed a nice man, Sarah thought as she settled back to listen to India's progress report. Very nice. She liked him a lot. It seemed odd that he was here alone. She wondered if that had anything to do with the problems to which India had alluded.

'Did you bring your car?' India asked Sarah at the end of the evening.

'No. I walked.'

'Can I give you a lift home, in that case?' Robert asked.

'Well . . .'

She almost said she could walk. She didn't mind walking on such a pleasant evening.

'It's raining now,' India added.

That seemed to settle it.

'Thank you,' she said with a smile. 'That would be very welcome, Robert.'

EXCITING NEWS

'This is it,' Robert said. 'My pride and joy.' The car looked old, very old. Sarah stared at it, uncertain about the colour scheme.

'You're wondering about the blue door panel?' Robert chuckled.

'Just a little. Are you rebuilding the car?'

'That's exactly what I am doing—when I get the time.' He opened the passenger door for her. 'Jump in. And don't worry—the roof doesn't leak!'

It didn't. And the engine started with a healthy roar before settling into a slow, powerful throb. Sarah glanced round and took in the wood panelling and leather trim. She found she could stretch her legs way out in front of her, which was rather agreeable.

'What make is it, Robert?'

'A Wolseley 14/60, one of the best cars ever made at their Ward End Works in Birmingham. One of the last, as well. They moved in nineteen forty-eight.'

Sarah sniffed. 'I can still smell the leather—even after all these years!'

'Petrol, too, on a really hot day. I still haven't found the leak. But the old thing gets me around—most days.

'Which way?' he asked, as they set off.

Sarah directed him and then asked if he had known India and Harry long.

'Years and years. They were just about our best friends. My wife and I, I mean.'

'Oh?'

He glanced at her and added, 'I'm a widower. Jenny died the other year.'

'Oh, I'm sorry! I didn't know. India didn't say anything.'

'It's all right. Don't worry. But, yes, we've all been good friends a long time. How about you?'

'India and I just met recently. It was very funny, actually.'

She told him about India's altercation with the parking warden. He laughed and slapped the steering wheel with one hand. 'That's our India! She'll never change!'

'But she soon recovered,' Sarah said. 'Tears to laughter in about thirty seconds. Then we had coffee.'

Robert glanced sideways, still chuckling. 'You were lucky to meet her on your first morning here. Some people have to wait years before they witness one of India's performances.'

'Yes,' Sarah said, laughing. 'I think even then I felt privileged.'

A minute later they were home.

'This it?'

'Yes. Aidan House. I have one of the new flats here.'

'I wondered what they were doing with the old place. Nice and handy for the town centre, eh?'

'It is, yes.'

He got out, came round and opened the door for her. 'Good to meet you, Sarah.'

'Thanks for the lift, Robert.'

'You're welcome. Take care now.'

She walked to the front door, key in hand, then she turned to give him a little wave as he departed. Nice man, she thought happily.

*   *   *

The next morning she lingered over breakfast, torn between happy thoughts of the night before and growing anxiety about the future. It had been a lovely evening at India's.

What fun they had all had! She smiled as she remembered some of the things that had been said. Harry had been wonderful. For a man feeling down on his luck, as he kept saying of himself, he was bearing up remarkably well. He was such a good match for India.

Robert, too, had been good fun. Such a nice man. And a widower. What a shame. It always seemed particularly sad when a family lost someone, especially a mother, so young.

She wondered what the children were like, and how they were coping. Quite well, she guessed, or Robert surely wouldn't have been there last night. All the same, he had a heavy load to carry.

And if his job was also in jeopardy that was doubly worrying. No wonder India had said he was a man with problems.

Inevitably, though, her thoughts turned to her own problems, and especially to the need to find a job. Time was slipping away. She had already used a significant part of the six months she had allowed herself to settle in and get on with things.

The trouble was, as she had told them all last night, she had seen nothing for which she could apply, never mind actually have a chance of getting.

Something like her old job would be perfect, but she was unlikely to find such a job in Alnwick. She had no formal qualifications either. In her old job she hadn't needed them.

She had simply grown up in the business. The Jacksons had wanted loyalty and long service. She had given them that, and in return had been well rewarded. What an old-fashioned arrangement that seemed now.

She smiled as she recalled her introduction to the firm all those years ago. Then, old Mr Jackson had still been alive.

He had looked at her at the interview, studied her, and said, 'You must have your hair cut shorter, Miss Hodgkin. Our customers don't expect to see long hair in this store.'

That had been the memorable highlight of the interview. Young Mr Jackson's contribution had been to ask about her previous experience, which at the time had been almost non-existent. But she had got the job. They must have seen something they had liked.

Jackson's was never short of applicants for their jobs. They were known to be a good employer, and they were a well-respected, long-standing firm that had been part of Newcastle longer than anyone could remember.

The hair-length comment had shocked her at the time, and infuriated her later when she thought about it, but she had said nothing.

She had wanted the job. So she had put up with it, and had her hair re-styled.

Now, of course, she could have taken the Jacksons to some sort of tribunal and claimed damages for something!

She might not have got the job, but she would have won a victory of sorts.

She was glad that it, and she hadn't been like that then, though. Old Mr Jackson had turned out to be a wonderful employer.

Kind, generous, appreciative, he had soon become her biggest supporter, and seen to it that she prospered within the company. And young Mr Jackson, Clive as she had come to know him, had been just as good to work for when he took over.

Not as astute a businessman perhaps as his father, but more in tune with the modern world, he had ensured that the company had kept going when many old firms had not.

Her own role in the family-owned furniture store had been behind the scenes. She had risen eventually to the dizzy heights of office manager, along the way doing everything required.

When she left, she knew Clive had spoken the truth when he told her she would be hard to replace.

But he had not attempted to stand in her way or bribe her into staying.

He had understood that it was time for her to move on, and had wished her well.

She sighed. She quite missed the old place. She missed the stability and the security of it. Maybe she should go back and see them all.

Who could tell? There might even be some sort of job for her there still if she couldn't find one here. It was worth thinking about. She couldn't go on being unemployed indefinitely.

*   *   *

The sound of the door buzzer brought her out of her reverie. She leapt up with guilt. What was she doing, sitting here daydreaming like this?

'You're not still in bed, are you?' India's tinny voice warbled through the intercom. 'I just bet you are!'

Sarah laughed and pressed the button to open the front door. 'Come on up, India!'

Then she opened the door of the flat and stood waiting as India clattered up the stairs.

'Not far now!' she called even before India came into sight.

Her friend appeared and sagged against the wall for a moment, mouth wide open to suck in oxygen. 'These stairs,' she gasped. 'They've made them even steeper since I was last here.'

'You poor thing. Come on in.'

India sat down at the kitchen table and allowed Sarah to make her a cup of coffee. 'I didn't wake you, did I?' she said. 'At least you're dressed. That's something.'

'Of course I am. Don't tell me, you've been up for hours. I know.'

India grimaced. 'Indeed I have. My house is full of people with absolutely no consideration at all.'

'No, it's not, India. You have a lovely family. Harry's wonderful and the children are charming.'

'Huh,' India grunted. 'Harry wonderful? Now I know you're joking.'

'I had a lovely evening, India. Thank you for inviting me. It was great.'

India smiled and relented. 'Good. It was nice, wasn't it?'

'Perfect.'

'What did you think of Robert?'

Ah! Sarah thought with amusement. Is that why you're here so early? I might have known.

'He seemed a very nice man. I liked him.'

'He's a widower, you know.'

'Yes. He told me.'

'He has two children, a bit younger than our two.'

'Oh? Coffee or tea?'

'Coffee, please. Did he come in?'

Sarah laughed. 'India! You're terrible. No, he did not come in. He drove me home, and dropped me off outside the flats. That's all.'

'Pity,' India said with a shrug. 'I was hoping for romance.'

'I'm going to pretend I didn't hear that remark.'

'Yes, that's probably best,' India grinned. 'Listen, why I've come round at this unearthly hour . . .'

'Is to find out how Robert and I got on after we left your house last night?'

'Well, that, too. But mainly because I wondered if you would like to come and see my new premises.'

'For the shop?'

'Of course.'

'Oh, I'd love to!'

India smiled with satisfaction.

'I was just wondering what to do this morning,' Sarah said. 'I'm sick of looking for a

50

job. I'm sick of shopping as well.'

India laughed. 'And sick of housework?'

'That, too, not that there's much here to do.'

'You really do need a job, my girl. You need to get out and meet people as well.'

'Now you're talking. I'm missing that. You like your coffee black, don't you?'

Sarah set coffee mugs on the table.

'Yes, and with lots of sugar.'

Sarah grimaced. 'I'll see if I can find some.'

'I can always make do with chocolate.'

'Don't start! I don't need a friend that likes chocolate, India. I would be better off with someone who has to think more about what they eat—someone who needs to diet even more than I do.'

'I think about chocolate a lot,' India said with a sigh.

'Tough! I don't have any, and I don't keep it.'

'Neither do I, not with teenagers in the house.'

'Teenagers, huh?'

'Teenagers.'

'I bet they're no worse than you!'

ANOTHER SUITOR

Afterwards they went to see India's new shop. 'You've rented it?' Sarah asked. 'Already, I mean?'

'Yes, I have. And paid the rent for six months. I used Harry's redundancy money. No turning back now.'

Sarah smiled. She admired her friend's energy and adventurous spirit. India was really going for it. India had found an empty shop in Curiosity Lane, just off Bondgate Within, one of the main shopping streets in Alnwick.

It was small, with a single bow window that had pebbled glass panes set in a wooden frame. The adjacent premises, also with a bow window, seemed to be empty, too.

'Nothing to do with me,' India said when Sarah asked about it. 'That's separate. It used to be a café.'

'Pity it closed. It might have brought you more walk-by customers.'

India shrugged and unlocked the door of her own shop.

'Bet I know what you're going to call it,' Sarah said.

'You do?'

'I do.'

India laughed, opened the door and led the way inside. 'I'm way ahead of you,' she said, pointing to a signboard waiting to be hung up. 'I've named it already.'

'*The Old Curiosity Shop,*' Sarah read out aloud. 'It had to be, didn't it?'

'Ever since I first spotted it. So,' India added, waving Sarah forward. 'What do you think?'

The shop was entirely empty. It was long and thin, stretching away into the distance. The walls were well-marked from previous shelves and other fittings, but they looked sound.

'It's lovely,' Sarah said, looking around admiringly. 'All it needs is a coat of paint. And some decent lighting, perhaps. Can you afford to do things like that?'

'Yes, I think so. I've got a start-up fund and a business loan from the bank.'

'My! You've certainly got a move on.'

They walked the length of the shop, with India pointing out things on the way. 'Maybe I'll make the far end into a storage area,' she said. 'And put up a partition wall to shield it.'

'Yes, you'll need somewhere to keep your stock.'

'There is a cupboard at the back where the toilet is, but it's not big enough for much stock.'

Sarah stopped and wheeled round. She laughed and shook her head. 'It's wonderful, India! You've done really well to find it. I'm so happy for you.'

'Yes, well,' India said dubiously. 'All I have to do now is find something to sell.' She relented, smiled and added, 'I'm so glad you approve, Sarah.'

'Oh, I do!'

She managed not to add a word of warning or caution, or a negative comment. It was too late for that. India had embarked on her venture. What she needed now was support.

But Sarah still had her doubts about how well the project would go. Was a shop like this really what a town like Alnwick needed right now?

On the other hand, how could you ever know until someone tried it?

'I'm going to start painting this afternoon,' India said.

'The walls?'

'All of them.'

'I'll help.'

'Oh, thank you, Sarah!' India beamed and added, 'That would be wonderful. Are you sure you've got the time?'

'At this moment in time, my dear, any distraction is most welcome,' Sarah said with feeling. She meant it, too. 'Job-hunting's not all it's cracked up to be. Anyway, it will put me in mind for the party tonight.'

'Party? What party?'

'Didn't I tell you? The other residents are having a sort of welcome party for me. At least, I think that's what it is.'

'What a wonderful life you single girls lead.'
'Don't we?' Sarah said, smiling happily.

*   *   *

The party had already started when Sarah arrived to a round of applause.

'Here she is!' John cried. 'We thought you were going to stand us up.'

'Am I late?'

'No, of course not!' Linda assured her. 'Come on. Let me introduce you to everyone.'

There were a couple of dozen people present, far more than Sarah had anticipated. It was a little daunting to meet so many new faces, let alone to try to remember their names. One or two were residents of the flats, but the rest were friends of either Linda or John.

'Isn't this fun!' Linda cried, ushering Sarah towards a drinks table.

'So many people!' Sarah said, laughing. 'Where have they all come from?'

'All over! Meet my friend, Jason.'

'Hello, Jason.'

'Sarah! So good of you to allow us to hold a party in your name.'

'Not much to do with me, I'm afraid!'

'I'm Jessie,' a tall, blonde girl said.

'Hello!'

'This music,' Jessie winced. 'It's John's choice, isn't it?'

'I think so.' Sarah winced with her and added, 'It's a bit loud, isn't it?'

'I'll get him to turn it down a bit.'

Jessie disappeared, giving Sarah time to take stock. She looked around and decided John wasn't into interior decor, or even into tidying up very much. Books and clothes seemed to be lying everywhere, interspersed with a myriad of ornaments and pictures that looked as if they came from a variety of foreign holidays.

'What do you think?' Linda asked. 'Of the flat, I mean.'

Sarah laughed. 'Lovely? Homely?'

'For a grown man, you mean?'

'No, of course not!'

But somehow the comments seemed appropriate. 'Even so,' Sarah added, 'I'm going to enjoy myself'

'Quite right, too.'

Linda turned and disappeared, soon to be seen again dancing with their host. Sarah smiled. It was good to see people enjoying themselves. She seemed to have spent an awful lot of time alone lately. Too much time. She moved on, meeting people and talking.

Later, John joined her.

'Do you have a drink, Sarah?'

'Yes, thanks.' She smiled and added, 'And thank you for the party. I'm having a lovely time.'

He smiled back. 'What else could we do for

a new arrival? Dance?'

She nodded.

They danced and they laughed for quite a long time. John had a way of turning everything into fun. 'I'm sorry the flat is such a mess,' he said suddenly, when they paused to catch their breath.

'Of course it isn't. It's lovely. I like it.'

'Really?' he asked almost anxiously.

She brushed his cheek with her lips. 'Really.'

He gave her a hug. 'That's a relief,' he admitted, almost as if he had been worried it had made a bad impression on her.

'It looks well lived in, unlike mine,' she added. 'I've hardly got my boxes unpacked yet.'

'I could help with that.'

'Open them and turn them upside down, you mean?'

'Something like that.'

'Come on,' she said. 'Let's dance.'

There was food, too, later. Sarah had no idea where it had come from, or how, but suddenly there were pizzas being carved into slices, the spicy scent of them filling the air.

Paper plates bearing chicken drumsticks and chorizo sausages were handed round. Glasses were re-filled. And, all the time, the music pounded and people danced. John shouted to her, and she nodded happily back to him.

SECOND THOUGHTS

John took her to a nearby Italian restaurant a couple of days later. She had assumed he would have forgotten his invitation, but not a bit of it. He turned up exactly on time.

'Ready?' he asked.

'Yes,' she said with some surprise. 'I think I am.' He looked at her, with head to one side.

'What?' she said defensively.

'You look wonderful.'

'Thank you, John.'

She smiled happily. It was a long time since anyone had said that to her.

'Walk or drive?' John asked.

'It's such a lovely evening. Let's walk.'

'OK. We can have some wine then, as well as see Alnwick at its best. This is the time of year I like most.'

'Have you lived here long, John?'

'A couple of years.' He considered. 'More even. Four, I think.'

'Like it?'

'I do now you've arrived!'

She laughed. 'I bet you say that to all the girls.'

'No. Only to you—and perhaps to Linda, as well.'

She laughed again and tucked her arm in his. *Vincente's* was busy. Even early in the evening it was pretty well full.

'My goodness,' Sarah said. 'Happy hour, is it? This must be a very popular place.'

'Just as well I booked a table.'

'Clever you!'

Not only had he booked, but he seemed to be well known and could even exchange pleasantries in Italian with the waiter who attended to them.

'How often do you come here?' Sarah asked when they were seated at last. 'A lot?'

'Whenever there's no food in the flat and the shops have just closed.'

'Most nights, then?'

He grinned. 'You know me so well.'

'Not really.' She smiled, knowing she was going to enjoy the evening.

'John, I haven't thanked you properly yet for the party the other night. It was lovely. I really enjoyed it.'

'That's good. Me, too.'

A plate of garlic bread arrived, and a bowl of olives. They were soon followed by a bottle of wine, and another of water. Conversation started. Sarah laughed from time to time.

In fact, she laughed a lot. John was a very amusing man. They entertained one another very well. The evening gathered pace. Time flew. Then coffee arrived.

Sarah glanced at her watch. 'Goodness! I wondered why we were practically the only customers left.'

'It's not that time already, is it?'

'I'm afraid it is.'

He yawned. 'Sorry. I had an early start today and I've got another tomorrow.'

'Come on, then. Let's go home. We've had a lowly time again.'

He smiled his agreement.

She offered to go halves with the bill but he wouldn't hear of it.

'Next time, then,' she said, strangely sure there would be one.

'Next time,' he agreed with a sideways grin.

They walked home along nearly deserted streets. Alnwick in mid-week. Peaceful. Tranquil even.

The scent of cherry blossom was in the air. A warm breeze carrying it everywhere.

They parted outside John's flat. Sarah gave him a kiss on the cheek. 'Thank you so much,' she said. 'It's been a lovely evening.'

He smiled and watched her climb the stairs. She knew he was watching, and at the corner she glanced back and gave him a little wave.

He disappeared into his flat. She smiled and continued on her own way, thinking how traditional they were.

*   *   *

Over the weeks that came they saw more and more of each other. John would visit, sometimes to ask her out for a drink or a walk, sometimes to ask her advice.

They dined out once a week, and a couple of times went to the Playhouse together. She cooked a couple of meals for him, and he even took to scouring the newspaper job adverts for her.

They were good together. Sarah appreciated John's company. She appreciated his attention, too. He was charming and amusing. She liked him a lot, and her feelings were reciprocated. It was good to be no longer alone so much.

Linda noticed, and commented with some amusement. 'Funny how you're the one John is always asking out these days. It used to be me.'

Sarah looked at her, surprised.

Linda laughed. 'Only joking, but I have noticed. Are you two going out together properly now?'

'Properly? Well . . . I'm not sure about that. But you're right. I do see quite a lot of him. He's such good company.'

'Well, there you are then.'

'There I am, where?'

'You're a couple, aren't you?'

Sarah chuckled happily.

'Good luck! He's a nice man, and I'm happy for you both. I'm pleased somebody around here is having a romance because I'm certainly not!'

'Oh, Linda! How can you say such a thing? You're out nearly every night of the week. I'm only out once in a while.'

'If you say so,' Linda said with a grin. 'Anyway, how's the job-hunting going?'

'As badly as ever. I've been thinking about going back to my old place, seeing if they've got anything for me.'

'In Newcastle? Oh, no! Don't do that.'

'Well . . .' Sarah shrugged. 'I'll have to do something soon. My money's running out. Maybe I could get a job back there and commute.'

'It's a long way, Sarah.'

She sighed. 'Well, I've got John hunting for jobs for me now. Maybe he'll find me something.'

'Especially if you tell him you'll have to leave otherwise!'

Sarah laughed. 'Oh, I can't do that.'

But she knew she would have to do something soon. She couldn't go on much longer being unemployed.

Then there was her relationship with John. Linda's comments had made her realise that was something else she needed to think about.

A PLEASANT AFTERNOON

Painting India's shop took more than an afternoon, despite India's optimism. It took two days of intensive effort. But at last it was done. They could roll up the sheets protecting the floor, collect the tins and rollers for disposal, and massage aching backs.

'You'd think there might have been some help from the male members of the family, wouldn't you?' India said wearily.

Sarah smiled. 'Not when one of them is job-hunting and the other has football on his mind. Men can only do one thing at a time, remember?'

India grinned. 'Well, we've got it done. And the joiner's coming tomorrow to put up the shelves. I'm so glad we've finished the painting. Thank you, Sarah. It wouldn't have got done without you. I underestimated the time it would take.'

'We make a good team.'

'Don't we?' India laughed and added, 'If Harry had been here there would have been big arguments by now. We're lucky he couldn't come.'

*　　　*　　　*

On the way home, Sarah wondered what else India had under-estimated, as well as the painting job. Starting a business from scratch had to be a big learning experience. You would only really know what it took when you had done it.

Oh, well. India was very brave, and resourceful. She would manage. And if she could help her any more, she would.

Now, though, she had to think again about what she herself was going to do. Helping India with the painting had been a nice distraction but she still needed to find a job.

She paused beside a small park and watched a couple of children kicking a ball between themselves and a man.

Shrieks of amusement and derision rent the spring evening air. As the man got ready to kick the ball back to one of the children, he slipped and landed on the ground, causing even greater mirth amongst the children.

Sarah smiled and was about to move on when she paused, realising with surprise that she knew the man. It was Robert, India and Harry's friend.

She called to him and waved. He turned, shaded his eyes against the sun and waved back. Then he walked over to her.

'Hello, Sarah! What are you doing here—spying on my training methods?'

She laughed. 'I didn't recognise you at first,' she admitted.

'In my athletic mode, you mean?'

'Well . . .'

'Or was it not until I was flat on my back?'

She grinned. 'I wasn't going to say that, Robert.' He laughed, turned and waved the children over. 'Oh, don't stop for me! You seemed to be having such fun.'

'They were. I don't know about me.'

The children arrived at a gallop.

'This is Jack, and this is Holly,' Robert told her. 'Kids, this is Sarah:'

'Hello, Holly, and hello, Jack!'

'Hello,' Holly said, all freckle-faced and cheery smile.

'Did you see him?' Jack, who was a little older, guffawed. 'Did you see our dad fall flat on his back?'

'I did, yes. Lucky he wasn't hurt.'

Not to be out-done, Holly, probably four or five, said, 'I wish I had a camera.'

'That's enough of that!' Robert intervened. 'So where are you off to?' he asked, looking at Sarah.

'Home. I've been helping India paint her new shop. We've finally got it finished after two days.'

'Good for you. We're off for an ice-cream now. I'm exhausted.'

'Huh!' Jack snorted. 'It wasn't even a real game.'

'It was real enough for me, young man,' Robert said with a wink at Sarah.

'Can you come with us, Sarah?' Holly asked.

'Me?' Sarah was taken aback. 'Oh, no, thank you. I have to get home. Besides, you three deserve some reward for all your effort.'

'Please!' Holly insisted.

'Yes, why don't you?' Robert asked. 'You deserve some reward for all your effort in painting those walls.'

'Painting's not hard work,' Jack objected.

'We do it all the time at school.'

'These were big walls,' Sarah told him. 'Very big.'

'Come on,' Robert urged. 'Join us.'

'If you really . . .'

'We do!' Holly intervened, taking Sarah's hand.

'Where are we going?' Sarah asked.

'Not far,' Robert told her.

'We're going to a new ice-cream shop,' Holly said.

Sarah glanced down at her and laughed. 'We are, are we?'

Holly smiled happily. She was a lovely little girl. Jack was a nice looking boy, too. She was blonde, and he was dark. Quite a contrast.

'It is new,' Robert confirmed. 'It's a *boutique* ice-cream parlour.'

'Really? What's that then?'

'I'm not altogether sure. Jack spotted it and wanted to give it a try.'

'One of the boys in my school has been,' Jack said. 'He says it's great.'

'Oh, well,' Sarah said solemnly. 'With a recommendation like that, you have to give it a try.'

'They make the ice-cream there,' Holly said, not to be out-done again. 'And you can watch them doing it.'

'Oh?'

Sarah caught Robert's eye, and smiled. 'We're in good hands,' she said. 'They seem to know all about it.'

'Oh, yes. They do.'

They arrived outside the ice-cream parlour. Through the window, Sarah could see it was very retro, very like places she had seen in old films and photos. With its cane chairs and tables, the latter with glass tops, it looked a real period piece.

'This place used to be an antiques shop,' Robert said, 'not so very long ago.'

'In its way, perhaps it is still?' she suggested.

'Yes!' He laughed. 'Come on. Let's give it a go!'

*   *   *

Everything inside was delightful. The furniture, the waitresses with little lace caps, Billie Holliday singing softly in the background—and, most of all, the ice-cream. It came in an astonishing range of colours and tastes.

The children spent ten minutes poring over the menus, interspersed with flying visits to a glass wall, on the other side of which ice-cream was being made. They were breathless with excitement.

'Boutique ice-cream,' Sarah read off the menu. 'That's a new one on me.'

'Me, too,' Robert agreed. 'But it seems to work.'

'It does, doesn't it?'

While the children were away from the table, watching ice-cream being made, she said, 'Thank you for inviting me, Robert. This is a lovely idea. Such fun!'

He seemed pleased. 'Thank you for coming. Holly, especially, is really pleased. I do my best, but . . .' He fell silent.

'How long is it since your wife passed away?'

'Three years, going on four. It was a car accident. A lorry crossed the white line and hit her head-on. There was nothing that could be done.'

'I'm so sorry.' She winced and added, 'It must have been very difficult for you, Robert, but you've: done very well. The children are lovely.'

'Thank you.' He smiled. 'I don't know what I would have done without them. We've helped each other.'

She nodded.

'How old are they?'

'Eight and nearly five.'

'Does it hurt to talk about it?'

'Not now, no. In fact, I should do more of it. We don't want to forget her. On the other hand, we have all had to move on, haven't we? Lives to live. Especially the children.'

'Of course. I understand.'

She smiled at him. Then her eyes caught the returning Holly, who was full of hard-to-suppress news about something.

'Sarah!' the little girl said breathlessly. 'The

68

strawberry ice-cream has all plopped on the floor! The lady . . .'

Then it was too much for her to contemplate, still less articulate. She turned abruptly and dashed back to rejoin her brother.

'I'd better go and see,' Sarah said, pushing back her chair.

'Oh, yes!' Robert agreed. 'Indeed. A catastrophe like that?'

*   *   *

Walking home later on, Sarah was still chuckling to herself about ice-cream all over the floor, and staff wading through it as they attempted to deal with the flood caused by a very big machine malfunctioning. The children had been agog!

As for herself, she couldn't remember the last time she had been so amused, especially when one of the waitresses whispered that it was all right to laugh because this happened quite often and was part of the entertainment.

As she was passing a garage, a little hand-written notice caught her eye. It was stuck to the inside of a window. *Temporary office help wanted,* she read. She studied it for a moment and moved on.

What she knew about cars and garages you could write on the back of a postage stamp. About all she did know was how to drive.

Still, she would mention it to India. Perhaps Harry might be interested. He must be getting desperate to find a job. Anything would probably do by now, at least for a time. Somehow it was hard to see India's craft shop being the answer to all their prayers.

A TRIP HOME

The bus to Newcastle took an hour. Sarah didn't mind. It made a nice change both to be going somewhere and to be doing it without driving. She hadn't been back to the city since her move to Alnwick.

She was looking forward to it. Coffee in Bainbridge's or rather John Lewis as it was now. And it had been for years.

She would never get used to that. For her, and no doubt for many like her, it would remain Bainbridge's, just as it had been for a century or more. Anyway, it hadn't really changed and it was still the department store she liked best.

So, coffee in Bainbridge's. How she wished India could have come with her. That would have been fun. But India was too busy. So that was that.

After coffee she'd have a quick look round to see what had changed in Northumberland Street. Everything, probably.

But nothing would have changed in Grey Street, of course. It hardly ever did there. Grey Street was perfect already. After that, she could call into the old place. See how they were all getting on without her. Meet some familiar faces. She gave a little shiver of delight at the prospect.

Or should she wait, leave it a bit and go in after lunch? That might be better. The mornings were always the busier part of the day. She might not be so welcome then. Clive had always said, 'Anytime, come in anytime you're in Newcastle,' but still . . .

She would do that, she decided. She would have lunch in the Café Royal perhaps, or Fenwick's, and then go in to see them at Jackson's. That would be best. No point causing a disturbance.

Besides, in the afternoon it would be easier to do some personal fishing, to see if there just might be some sort of job for her.

Clive would be surprised, but she was becoming desperate, and needs must. The travelling would be a problem, but it could be managed. Anyway, she wouldn't even think about that for now.

*   *   *

She had forgotten how busy it could be in Northumberland Street, the main shopping street in the city. It was absolutely heaving with

71

people.

Crowds were pouring in and out of Marks & Spencer, and Fenwicks, and even bigger crowds were moving in waves up and down the street itself. How ever did they all get here? And how would they get home again? If it came to that, why weren't they all at work? It didn't look as if she was the only one with no job to go to.

The morning passed in a dream. She wandered happily through the crowded streets, ventured into the new shops and her old favourites. She had another coffee in a smart little Italian place then moved on and bought herself a pretty scarf in a little shop next door. It was wonderful. Oh, how she missed the city!

After lunch she made her way to Jackson's, the last of the old, family-owned furniture stores. It was in one of the quieter streets off Grey Street, an elegant little lane that hadn't changed much since it was built about the time Victoria became Queen.

She paused at the corner of Grey Street and turned to look down the long slope curving away towards the quayside and the Tyne. How many times had she seen this view?

The beautiful stone buildings either side fit so well. They were just perfect. She smiled and turned to make her way towards the steps and up into the Jacksons' building, Coquet House,

The atmosphere inside was as nice as ever. She had always loved the elegance of the entrance hall, with its mahogany walls and ceramic floor. It was so beautiful, and so tranquil.

On into the store. She peered around with pleasure. It was quiet, of course, just as it always had been, and spacious. People moved around calmly and easily. There wasn't the crush here you always got in the department stores, or in Eldon Square and Northumberland Street.

It looked just the same, too. Well . . . perhaps not quite, not exactly the same. Things had been moved. There was a different arrangements of beds, for example, and a display of rugs she hadn't seen before.

The picture gallery seemed to have been moved as well. And a sign indicated that there was now a coffee shop in the basement. Goodness! But that was a very welcome innovation. Good for Clive.

'Sarah!'

She spun round. A familiar face was hurrying towards her dodging between the porcelain cabinets.

'Hello, Louise!'

'You've come to see us at last. How lovely!'

They met and hugged, and admired each other. Sarah laughed with delight. She was so pleased to see her old friend and colleague.

'And how's country life suiting you?'

'Fine, thank you. It's wonderful.'

'You look as if it is. You must be very

happy.'

'I am, Louise. I really am. And how are you?'

'Oh, there's nothing much wrong with me— nothing that a holiday in the Caribbean on a big yacht wouldn't fix.'

Sarah laughed again. 'Still waiting for your millionaire to turn up?'

'Definitely. One day I will be appreciated by the right sort of man, one with a lovely town house, and a grand house in the country, then I can leave all this behind.'

'Oh, Louise! You don't mean that. You'd miss the place too much.'

'That's so true, I'm afraid. Anyway, to what do we owe the pleasure? Anything in particular?'

'No. It's just one of my rare visits to the city, and I thought I'd pop in and see how you all were. There's been a few changes, I see,' she added, waving around.

Louise grimaced. 'Just a few—so far.'

'Opening a café was a good idea.'

'Yes.' Louise seemed less than excited. 'We'll get used to it, I suppose.'

'And is everyone still here?'

'Most of us. Peg's gone, I'm afraid. And Ellie and Mary, and a few others. Tom Hudson, too.'

'Oh?'

Sarah was surprised. None of the people mentioned had seemed to be of retirement age. She supposed they must have gone on to better jobs, or perhaps they had just fancied a change.

'Cathy's here, though. Are you going to see her? And Wilma, in Accounts.'

'I will, Louise. I'll look in on them. But first I'd better see if Clive's in. He'll go mad otherwise.'

'Yes, he's in. I just saw him half an hour ago. We could have a cup of tea afterwards, on my break?'

'Of course. I look forward to that.'

She made her way over to the staircase. She was so happy to see Louise again, but it had been a bit of a shock to hear that some of the others she had expected to see where no longer here. Still, things changed, didn't they? Times moved on, and so did people.

*   *   *

Clive's secretary, a new girl, smiled and ushered her into the inner sanctum. Clive himself wasn't looking as well as she remembered.

In fact, he was almost gaunt. His well-groomed hair a lot greyer now than it had been a few months' ago.

But his smile and affectionate welcome were as she remembered, and had hoped for.

'Sarah! How wonderful. Come in, come in!'

'Hello, Clive. I'm so glad I've found you

75

here.'

'Oh, I'm always here, you know me. Where else would I be? But you should have let me know you were coming. We could have organised a lunch for you?'

'Oh, no!' Sarah laughed. 'I wouldn't have wanted you to go to any trouble, but it's good to see you. I don't often come into the city, and I just thought I would call and see how you all were.'

'Well, I'm glad you did. Sit down, Sarah please! Kirsty, would you mind bringing a pot of tea for us? It's not often we have such a distinguished visitor.'

'Not at all, Mr Jackson.'

'He's exaggerating, Kirsty. Distinguished visitor indeed! I'm just Sarah. I used to work here?'

'I gathered that,' the girl said with a smile.

'So how is life in the far north?' Clive asked.

'Wonderful, thank you. Louise has just asked me the same question.'

Clive laughed.

'And you, Clive? How are you?'

'As you see.' He waved a hand in a self-deprecating way. 'A little older. None the wiser, though.'

Sarah smiled. 'The store looks as wonderful as ever. I was so happy to see it again. Some changes, though, I noticed?'

'Yes. Just a few.'

'And Louise told me some of the old gang

have gone. I'm sorry not to see them.'

'Yes,' Clive said, looking solemn for a moment. 'A sad business.'

'They'll be lucky to find better jobs than they had here.'

Clive nodded. 'I hope you're right, but I'm afraid there was no alternative. We had to let them go, I'm sorry to say. The recession has hit us badly, you know.'

'Oh, dear. Even Jackson's?'

'I'm afraid so. People simply decided they could do without new furniture, it seems. They're making do with what they have. A wise approach to economic uncertainty, I suppose, but it certainly hasn't helped us. I can't remember a time when we had to let permanent staff go. My father would have shot himself rather than have that happen.

'And goodness knows what Grandfather would have done. Taken a stick to the Prime Minister, probably.'

Sarah smiled, but she was shocked. She had never imagined such a scenario. Jackson's was part of the inner fabric of the city. The business had always been good and solid.

People never lost their jobs here if they were good workers, as her old friends had certainly all been.

'But we're still here,' Clive said with a renewed smile. 'There's plenty who can't say that. Ah! Here's our tea. Thank you, Kirsty.'

77

PAINFUL INDECISION

Oh, well, Sarah thought. That's that, then. There really is no going back. Clive had probably told her more than he had intended, or might really have wanted to tell her.

They were teetering on the edge, was what he'd said in so many words. The next few months would determine whether or not the century-old company would survive or bite the dust like so many others. He was desperate to avert more redundancies, but pessimistic about the prospects.

It was just as well, Sarah thought with a wry smile, that she'd not got round to asking if there was any chance of her getting her old job back—or any job for that matter.

That might well have sent poor Clive over the edge. As it was, he had seized on the reappearance of a familiar face, a sympathetic old-timer who knew so much about the business but was no longer connected, as a godsend.

He had needed to talk about his problems with someone without a direct interest, and there really were a lot of problems from the sound of things. He must be worried to death, poor man. No wonder he looked so gaunt and grey.

Now she was glad to be back on the bus,

heading away from it all. Her morning in the city had been very enjoyable, but by the end of the afternoon all she had wanted to do was escape. It hadn't been a mistake, exactly, to return to Jackson's.

She had enjoyed seeing the old faces again—those that were left, that is but enough was enough. She had problems of her own to face, and she had better get back home to do it.

While she was on the bus she phoned John. 'Meet me,' she said, 'and I'll buy you a pizza for supper.'

'Oh?'

'I've had a disappointing day, and I'd love to share it with you. Perhaps you'll make me laugh.'

'Well, you've made me laugh,' John said. 'So why not?'

'Can you get away early?'

'I'm away already—on a site visit?'

'Good.'

She switched off and smiled. Something to look forward to, she thought happily. How lucky she was to have a friend like John. He was even better in some ways than India.

You always had to be careful with India. You didn't want to set her off on an emotional rage about the injustices in the world—like not being able to find a job! John was much better.

Feeling more cheerful already, and looking forward to seeing John, she settled down to forget her disappointing day and enjoy thoughts of the enjoyable evening ahead. John, she thought happily. He was such a good man.

Always the same. Happy-go-lucky. She had never met anyone more that way. It was too soon to start wondering about where, if anywhere, their relationship was going, despite what Linda had said, but sometimes she did wonder, and always in a pleasurable way.

Relationship! She smiled. You couldn't call it that. Not really. Friendship was more like it. Still, she did like him, and he did seem to like her.

You could always tell when you kissed what someone really thought of you. On that basis, John liked her a lot.

She wasn't sure she felt the same, though. She did like him, but . . . well, she didn't feel about him as she had once felt about Marty. Romantically, that is. Early days yet, though, and it was far too soon to be thinking like that.

Enough! Enough for now, anyway.

She wondered if John really would be there waiting for her when the bus arrived. And he was. He wrapped his arms round her and hugged her. She giggled and protested.

'Well, I haven't seen you all day. Why the bus anyway? What's wrong with the car?'

'Nothing's wrong with it. I just didn't want all the hassle of trying to find somewhere to park.'

'Makes sense. So tell me about your day.'

'All in good time. Now, are you hungry?'

'Always,' he assured her. 'And there's a new restaurant I've spotted, one I haven't seen before.'

'Let's go there then.'

She hugged him and added, 'John, you really are a genius.'

'Moi?'

He fluttered his eyelids, and looked modest.

'Yes, you!' she said, laughing.

*   *   *

The next morning she went to see how India was getting on. Very well, was the obvious answer. The shop was set up and India was ready to go.

Sarah shook her head with admiration. 'It's beautiful!' she declared. 'You have a rare talent, my girl.'

'You think so?' India beamed with satisfaction. 'It's coming on, isn't it?'

'It certainly is! Now what do you want me to do? I've got a couple of hours to spare this morning.'

'Oh, thank you! I could really do with some help. Would you please check that crate for me? Make sure everything on the invoice is actually there.'

'And make the coffee?'

'And make the coffee!'

They laughed together and then got to

work. It had been the pattern for a while. Sarah dropped by most days to help, and there was always something to do, usually something urgent. They got on well together and Sarah knew how welcome her contribution was.

*   *   *

Over coffee a bit later, India said, 'You've been a wonderful help, Sarah. I'll never be able to thank you enough for what you've done.'

'Nonsense! Besides, we all need help at some stage in our lives, India. What are friends for?'

India smiled gratefully.

The big day was close now. The shop was to open on Friday and it was now Wednesday. India was becoming tense with expectation and apprehension.

'It will be fine,' Sarah assured her. 'It will be a wonderful day. You'll see.'

'I hope you're right.' India frowned. 'What if no-one turns up, though? What if I have no customers?'

'Then you can have a January sale.'

'In June?'

'Why not? The January sales seem to be starting earlier every year.'

India stared for a moment. Then she began to laugh. She laughed herself to the point where she was desperate for a tissue to blow her nose and wipe her eyes. Sarah just sat and watched, grinning.

'You should be on the stage!' India said eventually, when speech became possible again. 'Such a straight face that I believed you.'

'It will be all right on Friday,' Sarah repeated.

'Yes. Of course it will. How silly I am. Will you come?'

'I wouldn't miss it for anything.'

It was strange, and rather touching, Sarah thought later as she walked home. For all her extrovert personality, and her enthusiasm and self-confidence, India was vulnerable underneath.

In unfamiliar territory like this, she needed support and reassurance. She needed someone to be her mirror, someone to tell her how good she was. It was surprising, perhaps, in someone seemingly so confident.

But, then, she thought, was it really so surprising? She recalled how vulnerable Clive had been, and how he had welcomed the chance to tell her his troubles. Mind you, she admitted, Clive's troubles were a lot bigger than India's. If India's plans didn't work out, the shop would have to be closed and her suppliers would be owed money.

Perhaps bankruptcy would beckon. But that was all. She could walk away with her head held high, and get on with her life.

Poor Clive would think his life was over

if Jackson's went to the wall. Umpteen generations of forbears would be pointing their fingers at the man who had taken the family flagship down.

He would be as culpable as the captain of the *Titanic,* and remembered as such. At least, that would be Clive's fear.

Hopefully India's shop would do all right, though. Perhaps it wouldn't make much money. Quite possibly it might make a small loss. But it wouldn't be a disaster. At worst, it could only be a small disappointment. India need not be too fearful.

The pity of it was, of course, that it was only ever going to support India herself. It wasn't going to pay the wages for anyone else. It was too small. Otherwise she would have been interested in offering her own services. If only India had taken the premises next-door as well!

Never mind. Not to worry. When Friday was over, she would get back to concentrating on her own employment prospects, which at the moment were not much above zero.

As she was passing the garage, she saw that the notice advertising temporary work was still on display.

She hesitated, uncertain but suddenly curious. It was a garage. On the other hand, the work on offer was office work.

She stood still, staring at the notice for a moment. Then she turned and walked on to the garage forecourt.

AN OPPORTUNITY

She crossed the yard, dodging piles of used tyres and a car with the front end up high on a hydraulic jack. In the big, open barn she could see a couple of men manoeuvring the engine they were hoisting out of a truck.

Another boiler-suited man, this one wearing a big face mask, was wielding a welding torch as he worked at an oily bench. It was a busy place.

The office was tiny, little more than a little glass box at the back of the barn. Behind the cash desk a grey-haired woman with a stern, deeply-lined face was putting slips of paper on to a spiked pile.

'Yes?'

Sarah smiled tentatively. 'Hello! I was just looking at the job notice in your window, and wondering what it was about.'

'It's a temporary job. Here. For a month.'

'Doing what, exactly?'

'Doing what I'm doing now—doing everything, single-handedly!'

Sarah smiled but the woman didn't seem to be trying to amuse her.

'General office work?' Sarah enquired.

The woman snorted. 'If that's what you want

to call it. My husband thinks I do nothing all day, but if it wasn't for me . . . He just wants to spend his time chatting to folk about engines and what-not. Other people have to do the work.'

'Have I come at a bad time?' Sarah asked, beginning to regret the curiosity that had brought her in here.

'It's always a bad time in here.' The woman relented. 'What it is, we're very busy and I have to be away for a month. So we need someone to cover. That's all . . . Why, are you interested?' she added.

Sarah was cautious. 'I might be.'

'Know anything about cars and lorries?'

'Not really, no. Nothing at all, in fact,' she added, wishing she hadn't bothered making her enquiry in the first place. 'But I have worked in an office for a long time!'

'Where?'

'Jackson's, in Newcastle. It's a . . .'

'Furniture store.' The woman nodded to herself. 'So you know about cash and invoices, telephones, computers—and making tea?'

Sarah smiled. 'Just a bit,' she admitted.

'And you're interested in a temporary job?'

'Well, I do need a job.'

'Have you got a criminal record?'

Sarah was shocked. 'I beg your pardon?'

'We can't be too careful these days, where there's money involved.'

'Well, I haven't—and I'm not a silly young

thing either! I want to work and I've got the experience. And if you must know, I don't gamble or smoke!'

The woman smiled at last. 'You're just what we need,' she said.

'Maybe, but I'm not sure you're what I need!'

'Don't take offence, pet,' a man's voice said behind her. 'It's just her way. She's a bossy so-and-so.'

Sarah spun round. An elderly man with strands of white hair poking out from beneath an oily flat cap had appeared.

He was very dirty and scruffy, but he had twinkling blue eyes and a cheerful smile.

'I'm Ted Charlton,' he said. 'And this is my wife, Peg.'

'So who are you?' Sarah demanded, unappeased.

'This is *Charlton's Garage,* pet.'

'You mean it's your business?'

'From top to bottom,' the man said with satisfaction. 'Now, do you want the job?'

'Well . . .'

'You can start tomorrow,' Peg said. 'Seven-thirty sharp. One day for me to show you the ropes. Then you're on your own.'

'So soon?' Sarah gasped.

'I'm off to America for a month and we need someone here to make sure there's a business left for me to come back to.'

'It's the son,' the man said gently.

'Oh?'

Sarah's head was spinning. She didn't know what to think, or which one of them to look at and listen to either.

'He's thinking of getting wed out there.'

'The silly . . .' Peg began.

'Now then,' Ted said in a mild tone. 'It's his life.'

Sarah was beginning to feel a bit faint but she tried to rally. 'Where . . .?'

'Las Vegas,' Peg said with disgust. 'Little church wedding isn't good enough for him And he doesn't want anything to do with the family business.'

'Can't say I blame him.' Ted said with a wink at Sarah. 'If I had my time again . . .'

'In your dreams!' Peg said with a snort. 'All you're good for is changing tyres and fixing engines.'

'Aye, well. Somebody has to do it. He'll come round, Davey will. It might take a while, but he'll be back here soon enough when the money runs out.'

'I don't think she will be, though,' Peg said with a snort. 'She's bound to have more sense than him.'

'You've got something there.' Ted turned back to Sarah. 'Well, then, are you going to come and give us a hand?'

Sarah found herself saying yes, although afterwards she did wonder what she'd got herself into. But it had been such a dreadful

88

day that she didn't much care what happened next. And she needed to work. She still needed a job.

*   *   *

Before Sarah completed her journey home, she stopped to have a cup of tea at a little café where they always had the most wonderful cakes.

She needed some comfort food, and a cream cake with bits of chocolate in the middle would do nicely. She also needed to sit and think.

The past couple of hours had taken their toll. The last hour, in particular, had been almost overwhelming. She needed a job, though. She also felt she had to reconnect with the real world and that meant earning an honest wage.

She shook her head and gave a reluctant smile. The Charltons! What terrible people they were.

No, they weren't, she thought then with a wry chuckle. They were just . . . different! So it looked like she had an interesting month ahead of her. You never knew what was coming up in life, you just couldn't tell. This might be exactly what she needed. And even if it wasn't; the money would come in handy.

A SHOW OF JEALOUSY

While she was fumbling with her key to the door of her flat, the door on the opposite side of the landing opened.

'Hi, Sarah! I thought I heard you.'

'Hello, Linda.' She turned with a smile, holding the door open with her foot. 'I'm so tired. Oh, what beautiful flowers!'

'They are, aren't they?' Linda held the bouquet at arms' length and examined it critically. 'From Guernsey, apparently.'

'You must have an admirer.'

'Perhaps. I don't know, because the flowers aren't for me. They're for you.'

Smiling knowingly, Linda held the bouquet out.

'For me? Oh, I don't think so. Unless . . .'

She stopped, wondering if it could be another peace offering from Marty. But he didn't know where she was living. From John, then?

'Come on, Sarah,' Linda said, still smiling. 'Please take them. My arms are aching. I can't hold them any longer. And they're definitely for you. The man said so.'

'What man?' Sarah reached out to take the bouquet. She was even more confused than ever. 'John?'

'I don't know. You'll have to read the note.

Anyway, I have to fly. Got a date. See you!'

Sarah stood for a moment, the bouquet in her arms, listening to Linda clatter down the stairs. Then she shook her head and went inside.

Linda was right. There was a note. She opened it after laying the flowers down on the table.

Dear Sarah,

Just a small thank you for joining us the other evening. The children, especially Holly, enjoyed your company very much—and so did I!

Yours,

Robert.

She read the note. Then she read it again with a slightly incredulous smile on her face. After that she searched for something big enough to hold the flowers. She came up with a glass water jug.

Until she got round to buying a vase, it would do very nicely.

After that, she made herself a mug of peppermint tea and sat for a while, staring at the flowers and wondering what it all meant. Something or nothing? It had to mean something, surely? Robert had gone to some trouble to find them, and then to get them here.

She smiled. What a nice man. A nice family, she thought fondly. Perhaps she would see them again. She hoped so.

Meanwhile, she must get their phone

number or address from India and thank Robert for the flowers. They were quite unnecessary, of course. There had been no need at all for him to send her flowers.

Why had he? She could think of no real reason. Unless . . . oh, no! She mustn't think like that. It was simply a kindly gesture from a courteous man, that was all. It didn't mean anything else. Was he romantically interested in her? Not really. She mustn't read more into it.

Still, she was thrilled, charmed in fact. She sat and gazed at the flowers for a while longer and allowed herself to dream a little.

Then the door buzzer went. Who could that be? She glanced at the clock as she got up. That time already? Goodness!

'John! Come in.'

'Well, OK. But I was wondering if you fancied going out?'

'Oh, John! I've just got in. And guess what?'

He followed her inside. She led the way into the kitchen and reached for the kettle.

'Nice flowers,' he remarked.

'Aren't they? They were left with Linda.'

'Oh?'

'Guess what,' she said again. 'I've got a job!'

'A job? You never have?'

'I know, I know! Incredible, isn't it?'

'Where what and where?'

She began to tell him about her day as she made two mugs of coffee and helped herself to a slice of cheese.

'A garage!' John said, laughing. 'What on earth possessed you?'

'I can drive. I've got a car.'

'Yes, but . . . well, congratulations, I think. Is it what you wanted?'

'I wanted a job, John. I need a job. Otherwise, I can't stay here.'

'I see.' He eyed the flowers and asked, 'Who sent them?'

'Oh, just a friend. You don't seem very pleased for me?'

'Well, of course I am, if it's what you want. Good luck with it. Come on! Let's go and celebrate.'

'I haven't had anything to eat since this morning. I'm starving.'

'We'll get some fish and chips—or something. Anything!'

Laughing, she put her coat back on and allowed herself to be led away. John filled the stairway with his chatter and hoots of delight.

Such friends, she thought, as she clattered clown the stairs after him. She had such good friends.

A NEW JOB

It was only a ten minute walk to the garage, and Sarah was there before seven-thirty. That seemed a bit early to be starting work, but the place was in full flow by then.

The lights were on. Engines were revving. Pop music was playing on the radio in the barn where the mechanics were already banging and screeching. As she approached the door to the office, she could see both the Charltons conferring inside.

'Good morning,' Sarah called as she pushed open the door.

'Oh, there you are, pet!' Ted smiled a greeting. 'Come on in. We're just sorting things out for the day.'

Peg glanced up and said, 'I didn't expect to see you again.'

'You weren't expecting me?' Sarah asked with alarm. 'Did I get it wrong?'

'Take no notice of her,' Ted said with a chuckle. 'She's a bad-tempered old so-and-so at the best of times, and in the morning she's ...'

'I thought it would be too much for you,' Peg said, overriding her husband. 'Working in a dirty old place like this.'

'I need the job, Mrs Charlton,' Sarah said crisply. 'That's why I'm here.'

'Good. Come and get started.'

'I'll leave you two to get on with it,' Ted said. 'We've got a couple of big jobs on today. I'd better get the lads started.'

'It looks as though everyone is already working very hard,' Sarah said.

Ted chuckled. 'You know nothing about garages, do you? They're all doing something, but none of them wants to do anything difficult. They just want to cruise through till tea break.'

He sounded like a real slave driver, Sarah thought uneasily. She glanced at Peg and was reassured to see her wink. 'He thinks he's the boss,' Peg said in a stage whisper.

'And don't you forget it!' Ted warned before he departed.

Sarah gave an uncertain smile. She felt as if she had a lot to learn—not only about garages, but about the people in them, as well.

*　　*　　*

It was a busy morning in the office, as well as in the yard. Peg dealt with phone calls while she was making up wage packets and telling Sarah where everything was.

There was a lot to remember, all delivered at a rapid pace, but it was basic office work, and very little was new to Sarah. There was just a lot to absorb at break-neck pace.

'You'll soon get the hang of it,' Peg said more than once. 'And if there's anything you're not sure about, just ask Ted or one of the lads.'

The main problem, Sarah thought already, was going to occur when someone rang up and wanted to book their car in for a job she had never heard of. She was bound to get it wrong.

'I know what a wheel is,' she confided to Peg after one call, 'and I've heard of brakes and gears, and tyres, and things. But what's a *differential*?'

'When you've been here thirty years,' Peg said with a chuckle, 'you'll know more about cars than the manufacturers do. Until then, just ask!'

Sarah laughed. It was sensible advice, and she was starting to feel more at ease. Peg had watched and heard her doing things and seemed to trust her already, which was a big step forward.

'Shall I make the tea?' she asked after a couple of hours, seeing Peg start to assemble things for the mid-morning break.

'You? Can you make tea as well?'

'As well as answer the phone and sharpen pencils, you mean? Certainly I can. I've had a lot of practice.'

'My! You're a real find. Help yourself.'

Sarah smiled and got on with it. She was becoming used to Peg's sharp tongue and her sarcasm.

Beneath that gruff exterior, there was obviously a sharp intelligence and a great capability. Peg was no fool. Running this office on her own was a demanding challenge.

Over their mugs of tea, the older woman gradually released more about herself and the business.

'You see, Ted and I came from nothing, from nowhere. We had nothing at all when we started out. But we slowly built this place up, and now we have a good business and a good life. The garage is our life,' she added for emphasis.

'I can see that,' Sarah said. 'It's an exciting place, isn't it? The garage, I mean. So much going on all the time.'

Peg smiled warmly. 'I'm glad you think that, dear. Not many would. At least, they wouldn't think it's where a woman should be. Ted didn't, at first.'

Sarah glanced at her with a smile.

'But he needed help and couldn't afford to hire anyone. So I had to step in and I had to learn to swim in a man's world. Then we became a team, a real partnership.'

Sarah listened. She was fascinated by Peg's story. She had worked in offices all her working life, but never one like this.

She had worked in big offices, where people were specialised and structured—and numerous. Here, you did everything yourself. You were it! There wasn't anyone else.

'Who made the tea today?' Ted wanted to know.

'She did,' Peg said.

Sarah waited apprehensively.

'Ah! I thought it was a bit better than usual.'

'You can make it yourself in future,' Peg said. 'Sarah won't always be here, and I'm never doing it again if that's all the thanks I get.'

Ted gave Sarah a wink. 'How are you getting on?' he asked.

'She's getting on just fine,' Peg assured him. 'Now clear off!'

'It's a lot to take in,' Sarah said, 'but I'm doing my best.'

'That's all we can ask,' Ted said. 'We wouldn't expect anything more. Give a shout if you're not sure about anything.'

*   *   *

The pace seemed to slow in the afternoon. That wasn't surprising. The mechanics had broken the back of the work. The big jobs were well in hand. The little jobs were being ticked off.

The men were winding down. Customers were arriving to collect their cars.

Sarah worked with Peg on the invoices and bills. Cash came in. Cheques were written. The card reader worked overtime. Ted was in and out of the office with queries and fine detail about particular jobs.

'I'm going to struggle on my own with this end of things,' Sarah confided to Peg.

'Ted will come and help you sort it out. He knows it all like the back of his hand. Don't worry. You'll be fine.'

It was a vote of confidence that carried

Sarah through the remainder of the day. Soon the garage was quiet and the men were leaving. Lights were being switched off and the machines were falling silent. The yard was emptying, too.

'Get away home,' Peg said eventually. 'Me and Ted will do what's left.'

'Are you sure?'

Peg nodded. 'Thanks for coming in today, Sarah. You've done well. I can go off tomorrow with confidence this place will survive till I get back.'

'Thank you, Peg. And I hope you have a good trip.'

Peg grimaced. 'I'm not at all sure about what I'm going to be like when I get out there, but I have to go.'

'Ready, Sarah?' Ted said, coming into the office. 'I'll run you home!'

'Oh, no thanks, I'd rather walk. But thank you anyway. That's very kind of you.'

Ted smiled. 'Will we see you tomorrow or have you had enough of us already?'

'You'll see me tomorrow,' Sarah assured him firmly. 'I've enjoyed it today.'

'Really?' He looked surprised.

'She's a good girl, Ted,' Peg said, 'a very good girl. We're lucky to have found her.'

For once, Ted seemed unsure what to say to that. 'Get away home then, pet,' he said eventually. 'And thank you for coming in.'

Sarah smiled all the way home. It was a long

time since anyone had referred to her as a girl, or called her 'pet'. But she didn't mind at all.

HELLO AGAIN

On an impulse, Sarah went back out after she had had something to eat. She returned to the little park where she had seen Robert and the children playing football. They were there again.

'Do you come here every night?' she asked, approaching Robert.

'Sarah!' Holly shrieked with delight.

Robert turned to her with a smile. 'Hello! Well, just about, since the light nights returned.'

'Not in the rain, though,' Holly assured her.

'Softies!' Jack scoffed.

'No, we're not!'

'I didn't mean to interrupt your game,' Sarah said to Robert. 'I just wanted to thank you for the beautiful flowers. Not that there was any need for them!'

Robert just smiled. 'Glad you liked them.'

'I helped choose the flowers,' Holly said.

'Huh!' Jack said with a grin. Then he turned and took off dribbling with the ball, heading towards an open goal.

'Wait, Jack!' Holly screeched. 'That's not fair.'

Sarah laughed and turned to Robert.

'They wear me out,' he said, shaking his head. 'Always on the go, they never seem to stop.'

'They're lovely children. You always seem to be having such fun.'

'Yes, I suppose we do. What about you? Much fun today?'

'Oh, yes! Today was something special. I started a new job.'

'Really? Tell me more.'

So she did. She told him all about her day, and how she was tired but pleased she had coped.

Robert shook his head and chuckled. 'Well done!' he said. 'I know that garage and the couple that run it. They're a right pair.'

Sarah agreed. 'But they're very nice, really,' she said. 'A bit tough, perhaps, but they've probably had to be.'

'I'm sure they have. It must be a tough business, running a garage. Anyway, we're about finished here. Walk home with us? You go past our road, don't you?'

*   *   *

Sarah walked back with them and when Robert invited her in for a cup of coffee she was happy to accept.

The house was in a quiet street of big Victorian villas, that had a small garden at

101

the front and a yard at the back. The entrance porch had an inner door with stained-glass windows and a tiled floor that featured a sunburst.

'Oh, I do love these old houses,' Sarah said, admiring the floor tiles and the glass.

'What? These draughty old places with all their gloomy rooms?'

'Well,' she said, as they moved through into the kitchen, 'what I see is lovely big rooms with fine decorative features. How many rooms, incidentally?'

Robert squinted at her. 'I don't know. I'm not too sure actually. I'd have to count them. Anyway, it depends what counts as a "room". The back scullery, for instance. Do we include that?'

Sarah smiled. 'You tell me.'

'We have four bedrooms. Perhaps that's the best guide.'

'Come and see my room?' Holly cried, coming into the conversation.

'Not now, Holly!' Robert said, laughing. 'We've only just got in the house. Later.'

She pouted for a moment and then dashed off to join her brother who was operating something that made a lot of noise.

Robert advised Sarah that it was a toy much promoted on television, one of which she had never heard.

She shrugged helplessly. 'That's a new one on me.'

'It was on me, too. The kids spot these things on television, and then they draw up their wish lists.' Robert shook his head and grinned. 'I can't keep up with them!'

'I'm not surprised?'

'Coffee, or tea?'

'Tea would be nice.'

'Sit down, sit down, it won't take a minute.'

She sat on a dining chair and gazed around. The kitchen was a comfortable, welcoming room. That went well with Robert and the children.

She felt very content here. Even though she hadn't known them long, she felt comfortable with this family. The children were lovely and Robert was such a charming, handsome man.

'I take it you don't have previous experience of working in a garage?' Robert said, as he waited for the kettle to boil.

She chuckled. 'None at all. They were desperate, I think. They needed someone at short notice and there I was. It's just for a month or so anyway.'

'What did you used to do? You moved from Newcastle, didn't you?'

She nodded. 'I worked in the main office of a family-owned furniture store in the city. Jackson's. Perhaps you've heard of it?'

'Oh, yes. Of course. They're quite famous, aren't they?'

'Yes, they are. Anyway, I was the general office manager, having worked my way up from making the tea and licking envelopes and stamps.'

'So you were there a long time?'

'I was. Too long, really.'

'Is that why you left?'

'No, not really. I liked it well enough. I moved for more . . . more personal reasons, really.'

'I'm sorry. I didn't mean to pry.'

'No. That's all right. I was in a long-term relationship that came to a natural end. I needed a new start and a complete change of scene!'

'And somehow you ended up in Alnwick!' Robert smiled and filled the tea pot. 'Lucky us!'

SETTLING IN

Once again the garage was in full swing when she arrived on the second day in her new job. She took a deep breath. This was the big one, the first day on her own.

Ted was in the office, doing bits and pieces while he waited for her. 'Good morning!' he boomed.

'Morning, Ted. I'm not late, am I? Peg said seven-thirty. Was that wrong?'

'No, no! Seven-thirty is perfect for in here. Some of us can't sleep, that's all. And if I'm awake, I might as well be here as sitting around the house.'

Sarah smiled. 'So you're all insomniacs here?'

Ted laughed. 'You know where things are, don't you? I'll leave you to get started. You don't want me in your way. But if you need anything, give me a shout.

'I'll take these job sheets with me,' he added, gathering a pile of papers.

She was relieved to be left alone. She needed to gather her wits and make a start, flying solo.

Within thirty seconds the phone rang. 'Good morning,' she said crisply. 'Charltons of Alnwick.'

'I want to speak to Peg,' a gruff man's voice said.

'I'm afraid she isn't here. Can I help?'

'And who might you be?'

'Sarah. I work here. Can I help?'

'No, you don't work there. Peg's the only woman in that place. I've been coming there for twenty years. You can't tell me . . .'

'I'm very busy, sir, but I would really like to help you,' she said firmly. 'What can I do? Or do you want me to fetch Mr Charlton to speak to you?'

'Oh, the no-nonsense type, eh?' The man chuckled. 'Good for you, pet! You must have been trained by old Peg. I'm ringing about my truck. Is it ready yet? I need it.'

'Nothing's ready right now. Our day has just started. But if you give me your name, I'll find out when it will be ready and ring you back.'

'Your day's just started?' he said incredulously. 'You lot want to try farming! That would wake your ideas up.'

Ted returned just as she put the phone down.

'A Mr Armstrong, from a farm near Chatton, just called.'

'Oh, him. Did he give you a bit of lip?'

'Not really. But he thinks we should start work earlier.'

Ted chuckled. 'That's him! He's a grand fellow to have on the phone first thing in the morning, isn't he? Don't mind him, though. He's not the worst customer we have. At least he pays his bills on time.'

'He wants to know if his truck's ready.'

'After dinner, tell him. It'll be ready by two this afternoon. He can collect it any time after that.'

'I think he wants it now,' Sarah said with a smile.

'They all do, all our customers. You'll have to grow a thick skin, sitting at the end of that phone. If he starts complaining, just tell him we'll fetch Peg back from Las Vegas to sort him out!'

So she was off and running. The working day had started. She was soon fully immersed in the life of the garage, and starting to

106

appreciate how capable and resourceful Peg must be.

The queries, the phone calls, the orders to write, the cheques to place carefully aside, the parts to order . . . and then there was the tea to make!

The morning flew past quicker than any she could remember. At twelve-thirty Ted returned and told her to take a half-hour break for lunch.

'I forgot to suggest you bring a sandwich, or something. If you haven't brought anything, there's a man with a van comes round about now. You can catch him.'

He dug into a pocket in his overall and extracted a screwed up five-pound note that he offered her.

'It's all right, thank you, Ted. I've brought something.'

'It must have been through the washer,' he said, before pushing the bank note back where it had come from. 'I'll have to tell Peg when she rings up.'

'She'll be pleased about that,' Sarah said with a grin.

'Perhaps I'll not tell her, then. We'll keep it to ourselves.'

'It might be best.'

He gave her a wink and left her to it. She smiled to herself and shook her head.

* * *

After eating the sandwich she had brought for her lunch, Sarah announced that she would go for a walk for ten minutes.

'Aye,' Ted said with approval. 'You'd best do that. Otherwise it'll be dark, and you'll have missed the day.'

It was sunny outside, she was surprised to find. That was going to be a problem with working in the office. There wasn't a great deal of natural light found its way through the grimy little window. But you were so busy, you didn't really notice. She would soon get used to it, she decided. And if she found time, she could give the window a polish.

Overall, she had quite enjoyed the morning. It had been good to be stretched in the way you were in a new job. And most people had been respectful and appreciative. On the whole, it seemed a good place to work.

She walked round the industrial estate, noticing businesses and activities she hadn't realised went on in the town before. It was an interesting area. Wholesale food depots. Tractor repair places. 'Country Life' clothing outlets. Even a fishing-rod factory. All sorts of things.

She saw the man who came round with the van selling sandwiches. He seemed to be doing a good trade. She saw him in a couple of places, and each time there was a queue of people waiting to be served.

That started her thinking about the former café next-door to India's shop, and wondering if there might be an opportunity there.

Perhaps it could be re-opened? She had never worked in catering, but it couldn't be that difficult. Plenty of people did.

It was something to think about. As she had said to India, a café there might increase the trade for the shop. The two businesses together could complement each other. She and India could even be a partnership? Separate businesses, or even one business with two owners? Why not? It was certainly worth considering. When her month here was over she was still going to need a job.

As she re-entered Charltons' yard she bumped into the foreman. Greg, she'd been told he was called. He was a big, quiet man who seemed to take his responsibilities very seriously. At least, she hadn't seen a smile on his face yet, even though he had been into the office several times to ask her to order parts.

'How are you getting on?' he asked.

'Fine, thank you. But it's really busy, isn't it?'

'Always,' he said. 'It's never been any different.'

'Have you worked here long?'

'Since I left school. Ted keeps people on if they do the job right. If they're no good, or mess him about, he soon sends them on their way.'

She nodded and wondered if this was leading anywhere, or if he was just being friendly. Perhaps it was a stern warning?

'You needn't worry, though,' he added. 'You're doing all right.'

'I'm glad you think so,' she said with a smile. They parted and she was still smiling. Greg had meant well, presumably, but the advice was a bit over the top for a one-month temporary job while the usual incumbent was away in Las Vegas. Men! They did take themselves so seriously at times.

BREAKING A BOND

'How's the new job?' Linda asked. Sarah paused at the top of the stairs and sagged against the wall.

'I'm shattered!'

Linda laughed. 'You're out of practice, that's all.'

'You're right, but it's good. Very busy, but interesting.'

'It's very brave of you, working in a garage. I couldn't do that. I know nothing about cars.'

'Neither do I, but there's plenty of people there who do.'

'Any handsome mechanics?'

'One or two. They're a bit grimy when I see them, but I'm sure they'll scrub up nicely.'

Linda laughed. 'You won't find a nicer one than your John. I'm so pleased for you, Sarah. I can see you're so happy, and I know John's very happy, too.'

'Is he?'

Linda winked. 'From what he tells me, and what he doesn't, I think he's making plans. He's going to surprise you one of the days. Oops! Excuse me.' Linda put her hand across her mouth and added, 'I don't think I should have said that.'

Sarah sat in the kitchen for a little while, elbows on the table, head in her hands. She stared at the wall opposite, and wondered why the clock had stopped. The battery, probably. She would have to buy a new one, or a pack of new ones. The spares would come in handy. You always needed batteries.

She roused herself and got up to make a pot of tea. She wasn't hungry but she made herself a salad sandwich to go with it, and then watched it grow stale, untried.

She sighed. This was no good. The conversation with Linda had upset her, frightened her in a way, but it had also served as a warning. What, really, was she going to do about John?

Linda had made her realise she needed to step back and think about where she was going, and what she was doing. How could she have been so blind—and stupid? John was such fun, and so happy-go-lucky. It hadn't occurred to her that he might take things so seriously. It just hadn't.

Take a deep breath, she advised herself. Think about it. John. He was lovely. He really was. Kind, bright, intelligent, fun to be with. What was wrong with taking it seriously? Maybe he was the one, the man she had been not looking for exactly but hoping secretly she would one day find.

But he wasn't. She knew that.

As soon as she asked herself the question she knew it wasn't like that for her. John was fun to be with, and a good friend, but he wasn't the man with whom she wanted to spend her life.

Then who was?

Maybe nobody, she thought miserably. Perhaps that man didn't exist. All she knew was that she wanted someone more like . . . well, like Robert, someone who made her shiver whenever he came near. Stop! She wasn't going to think about Robert. He had his life, a good life, and she wasn't part of it.

She smiled ruefully and got to her feet. There was no point in this, going round and round in circles. She had to get out. She would drive herself mad otherwise.

She had to hope things would sort themselves out in time, and that time would answer all her questions and uncertainties. Meanwhile, perhaps she could avoid seeing quite so much of John.

And then the worst thing happened. She encountered him in the hallway. There he was, full of light and cheer, as usual. And also as usual, he wanted her to go somewhere with him. She shook her head, tried to be careful with what she said, and couldn't manage it.

All her thoughts and feelings came out in a rush, as she tried to spare his feelings and yet tell him they had no future together.

It was impossible. He stood and stared, and she had never felt more miserable.

'Maybe you'll change your mind?' he said.

She shook her head. 'I'm sorry, John, but I don't think so. When I came here I had just got out of a long-term relationship that didn't work for me. I don't want to be in another one. I just thought we were good friends, not . . .'

'And so we are!' he said brightly. 'Good friends. Come on! Let's go out for a drink.'

'Not tonight, John. Thank you. I'm worn out. This new job . . .' she added vaguely.

'Yes, of course. That's why you're a bit down in the dumps. Another night, then?'

'Perhaps.' She tried to smile, and added, 'Maybe Linda would like to go out tonight?'

'Yes,' he said. 'That's an idea. I'll see what she says.'

She hoped that was the end of it. It was a pity, but she really didn't want to be in another relationship going nowhere. That wasn't why she had uprooted herself and come to Alnwick. From now on, she would just concentrate on the job. That was more than enough for her.

'IT'S BEEN A LOVELY EVENING'

Afterwards Sarah went round to India's shop. She had to have a change of scene, and there were bound to be last-minute things to be done there still. But there weren't many, she discovered. India was pretty much on top of it.

Sarah shook her head with admiration. 'You're ready!' she declared.

'Just about,' India agreed with a smile.

'Is there anything at all left for me to do?'

'Well . . . you could make a pot of tea, if you really want to help?'

'Oh, yes! I could. I'm good at that after the last couple of days.'

'How's it going?'

'The job?' Sarah laughed. 'Very well, actually. It's interesting and busy. The day just flies by.'

'I bet. Do you know a lot about cars?'

'I do now, and by the time Peg comes back I'll be able to go on *Mastermind*, my specialist subject will be cars. Do you know what a drive-train is, by the way, or a transmission? A few more days, and . . .

'You'll have oil all over your hands!'

'It could happen.'

114

'Perhaps you should start your own garage?'

'Only if you'll help.'

'Would I have to get my hands covered in oil, as well?' India shuddered at the thought.

'No, perhaps it wouldn't be a good idea.' Sarah grimaced. 'You might break a fingernail, as well. I'd better let you off. Anyway, you have enough to do here.'

India's big day was so close now they could touch it.

'What a pity I can't be here for your opening, India. I'm so sorry about that.'

'I'll manage. Harry will come to give me a hand. After that, he says, I'm on my own. He's still looking for a job, by the way.'

'No luck, eh?'

India shook her head. 'No, unfortunately.'

'They're short-handed at Charltons, in the workshop. The foreman was saying they need one or two extra men. I don't suppose he'd be interested in that, would he?'

'I don't know. I can ask him. To be honest, Sarah, I haven't got time or energy to spend on Harry's situation. The shop has just consumed me lately. Maybe it will be different after I open, but right now I'm so apprehensive.'

'It will be fine,' Sarah assured her. 'It will be lovely. You'll see.'

'I hope you're right. If you're not, I'm going to sue you for false promises.'

They got back to work, sorting out more stuff for shelves that were already groaning.

'Maybe we should stop?' Sarah said. 'Less is more, and all that.'

'Do you think we're putting too much on display?'

'Well . . . we want people to be able to see things, don't we?'

India laughed. 'I take the point. Perhaps we should stop. Now, what else is there to do?'

The doorbell rang.

'Who's that?' India wondered aloud. The door opened. 'Oh hello, Robert! Have you come to see how we're doing?'

Robert stepped inside and peered round. 'My!' he said. 'Isn't this wonderful? Hello, Sarah. How are you?'

'She's exhausted,' India said. 'She doesn't look it, but she must be. She's been up since first light.'

'Not quite.' Sarah chuckled. 'Hello, Robert. Have you got Holly and Jack with you?'

'Not this time. Someone is looking after them for an hour or two. Well, I must say, India, I'm really impressed with your shop. It looks wonderful. Not what I expected at all.'

'Thank you, Robert. We're nearly finished here. I just have a couple of bits of paperwork to do.'

'Should I start?' Sarah began.

'No, dear.' India shook her head. 'You should leave me to it. If you don't mind, that would be best. You just get away home. I can manage.'

116

'Well, if you're sure?'

'Take her away, Robert! Please.'

'Come on,' Robert said, laughing. 'We're both in the way. Let's go. Tell Harry I'll be round to see him one of these nights, will you?'

'If I remember. Good night!'

It seemed to Sarah that India wanted rid of her. In fact, she thought with a smile, she seemed to want rid of them both.

'We're not wanted,' she said to Robert.

'Evidently,' he said with a smile.

She felt better then than she had all evening. 'Have you eaten?' Robert asked.

'I had something earlier before I came to help India.'

'Something?'

'Just a quick piece of toast.'

'I was planning on visiting a little Italian bistro-type place just along here. Will you join me?' he asked.

'I'm not sure,' she said hesitantly.

'A few olives and a glass of wine, perhaps? A pizza?'

She looked at him.

'Please,' he said quietly. 'I would really appreciate it.'

Her heart skipped a beat. Why not, she thought. Why not, indeed!

She smiled her assent. 'That would be lovely, Robert. I must warn you, though. It's been a long day. If you see me falling asleep just prop my eyes open with matchsticks.'

'You don't think my sparkling wit could do the job?'

'That's an option,' she agreed, laughing.

*   *   *

It was a small restaurant in a place that used to be a shop, and before that the front room of a house.

Not, in other words, custom built. But it was pleasantly furnished and decorated and Pavarotti was in full voice somewhere in the background.

Sarah was surprised to find Robert had booked a table.

'Is it so popular that you have to do that?' she asked. 'Even during the week?'

Robert nodded 'Tell her, Luigi.'

The waiter laughed. 'Always,' he said, 'it is necessary. No man would want his wife or his girlfriend to be disappointed, just because he had failed to make a booking.'

Despite that, the restaurant was not crowded on this occasion and the atmosphere was very relaxed.

'Nice,' Sarah said with approval, looking around. 'Do you know, this is the first time I've been here.'

'Is it? Well, let's hope you don't regret it. I don't think you will, though. I come here fairly often. Usually I bring Holly and Jack. Luigi makes a big fuss of them.'

'And they feel very grown up?'

'Very.' He grinned.

'So why not tonight?'

He hesitated, looked down at his plate and then back up at her. 'To be honest,' he said, 'and I might as well be honest, I wanted to see and talk to you without them present.'

'Me?' she said, feeling faint.

He shrugged. 'I like you,' he said simply. 'Very much. I don't get out a lot these days, and I thought how nice it would be, just for once, to have the company of a beautiful and interesting woman without having to break off every two minutes to wipe a runny nose or nip a quarrel in the bud.'

He looked away and then back at her, then shrugged. 'I know it was presumptuous of me to book a restaurant, but . . .'

'Stop, Robert,' she said gently. 'Don't explain any further. It was a nice thing to do. I'm very pleased.'

He looked relieved.

She said, 'Shall we order?'

'How's the job going?'

'Well. It's busy, but I like that.'

'You do?'

'Yes. Today was my second day there, but my first without Peg to hold my hand. So it was sink or swim.'

Robert smiled. 'Everything's new to you?'

'Everything! Now I'm exhausted, but I enjoyed it. I really did. Perhaps it's just that

I'm not used to doing nothing all day. The Charltons are a funny old couple. I was appalled at first, some of the things they say to each other. But I soon realised they're a good team. They've built that business up from nothing. It's taken them many years but they've done it, and they're very proud of their achievement. It's their life's work.'

'See if they've got a job for me.'

She smiled. 'You'd have to be prepared to get your hands dirty. It's not like working at a desk in County Hall, you know.'

'Maybe I could look after new cars? Let you handle the old and dirty ones.'

'I don't think they see many new cars at Charltons. But if you want to keep an old one on the road, that's the place to go. You should see the state of some of the cars and the pick-ups the farmers bring in! One way or another, though, Ted and the lads seem to get them fixed and back on the road.'

'It's a rare talent, fixing things,' Robert reflected. 'People used to do it all the time. Now we just throw stuff away and buy new.'

Their wine arrived, followed closely by their food. 'This is lovely, Robert,' Sarah said. 'Thank you so much for inviting me.'

'I'm happy you could come. It makes a nice change for me.'

They smiled happily at one another. Then Robert added, 'The children will be jealous that I've had you all to myself this evening.'

Unthinking, she placed a hand on his and said, 'Don't tell them then.'

'Our secret,' he said, gently squeezing her hand.

Sarah's head began to whirl. Afterwards, she realised she had no idea what she had eaten that evening. All she could recall was that had spent it with Robert, and it had been wonderful.

Not exciting or uproarious, like evenings with someone like John could be, but just . . . wonderful. Perfect. Exactly how she would like her evenings to be.

*   *   *

Walking home afterwards, Sarah slipped her arm into Robert's, and it seemed the most natural thing in the world.

She loved being with him, having him beside her. She knew, too, that he was just as happy to be with her. Strange, but you always knew when things like that were true. Even before the first kiss.

'It's been a lovely evening, Robert.'

'Hasn't it just? What luck I found you at India's.'

She smiled and then said, 'Was it really? Was it luck?'

He chuckled. 'Whatever do you mean?'

'Oh, I don't know. Perhaps it was fate, something like that?'

He shook his head and stopped to turn her round to face him. 'No,' he said. 'I have a confession to make.'

'Whatever could that be?'

'I hoped you would be there.'

'Oh, really?'

She smiled. Even when he leaned down to kiss her the smile never left her eyes.

When they reached her flat, Sarah said, 'Would you like to see my flat? I think we should have a talk.'

He hesitated.

'Come and see where I live. Have a coffee.'

'I will. Thank you.' He glanced at his watch and added, 'I can't be late, though. I promised the child-minder I wouldn't be out too late.'

'No problem,' she said with a smile. 'Just a quick coffee.'

MORE GOOD NEWS

There were big problems at the garage. 'What's wrong, Ted?'

'Morning, Sarah. We're three men down, three of my best men, and we have a couple of big jobs to finish. I'll have to pick up the tools myself today. There was a phone call as well, from Peg. She says she'll have to stop longer. Her son's taken ill so the wedding's been put back. Can you stop on with us a bit longer, do

122

you think, Sarah?'

'Of course I can. What about the men who are missing?'

He listed the three. 'Crashed their car last night. Broken this and broken that.' He shook his head. 'You'd think they'd know better, wouldn't you?'

She assumed late-night frolics had been involved. 'Boys will be boys, unfortunately,' she said quietly.

'Aye. You're right. Now I'll have to go hospital visiting, but these jobs have to be finished first. I'm going to have to leave you to do everything in here yourself. Can you manage?'

'Why aye, man!' She gave him a grin. 'You'd better go and see if you can remember how an engine works, Ted.'

He chuckled. 'What a thing to happen, eh?'

But he went off cheerfully enough. She suspected he would enjoy himself, wielding a spanner again.

There were customers to call, parts to order, bills to pay and that was all before the tea had to be made. She got on with it and time flew by.

Just after ten she got an unexpected phone call. 'It's me. How are you?'

'India! I'm fine, thanks. How are you? Still busy?'

'A bit more comfortably busy now the bargain hunters have disappeared. But, yes, the shop's doing very well.'

'That's good.'

'I do miss our morning coffee together, though,' India said wistfully.

'Me, too,' Sarah chuckled. 'It's busier than ever in here. I could do with an hour over a nice cup of coffee right now.'

'In that case, I'd better let you get on.'

*   *   *

'I've been talking to Peg again,' Ted said a couple of days later.

'How is she?'

With the phone tucked between her cheek and her shoulder, Sarah listened to Ted and continued filing slips of paper, while she waited for the man at the other end of the phone line to decide whether he wanted to go ahead with the work on his car or not now he knew how much it would cost.

'Oh, Peg's all right. Nothing wrong with her. In her element, I should think.'

'And your son?' she added. 'How are things going? Is he any better?'

Ted sighed. 'I can't make out what's going on. He's fit enough, I think, but Peg says she thinks he's having second thoughts about this girl.'

Sarah gave a sympathetic wince. She knew how it felt to feel trapped.

'You do?' she said into the phone. 'Good.

124

Next Tuesday all right for you? Thank you, Mr. Jackson!'

She put the phone down. It rang again immediately. She picked it up.

'Actually, any future wedding won't be happening, Peg says,' Ted said with a sigh.

'Oh? That's a pity.'

'It is, and it isn't.' Ted considered and added, 'So Davey's fickle. That's why I didn't go out there with Peg. I wouldn't have got a word in. Not the first time Davey has one of his spur of the moment ideas.'

'Yes, Mr Arkle. We're open from seven-thirty. Thank you. We'll see you next Tuesday.'

'Peg says she wants to stay out there a bit longer,' Ted continued, as if nothing was happening but his conversation with Sarah.

'Well, if your son needs her, she should. It's not an easy situation, is it?'

'In a way, it's brought things to a head,' Ted said. 'She'd been talking about it for a while.'

'What's that?'

Sarah scanned the inbox on her computer, not bothering with most of them. 'There it is!' she exclaimed. 'That's the one I've been waiting for.

'Your brake pads for the Volvo,' she explained. 'They've got them in at last.'

Ted grunted. 'It's taken them long enough. She's not getting any younger, you know.'

'Who? Peg?'

He nodded.

'What a cheek! Neither are you.'

He grinned. 'She's been on for a while about having a bit more time for herself. I'm happy enough. This place is where I want to spend my time, but Peg's different.'

'Being a woman, perhaps?'

'Aye. That comes into it, I expect.'

She clattered the keyboard. 'Yes, please!' is what we say to them, I think.'

'Who's that?'

'Smithson's. They want to know if they can come next week to look at that problem with the power supply. ASAP, I told them originally. They don't need to be so cautious and deferential now.'

Ted nodded. 'So what do you think?'

'About what?' she said absently. 'Is that the mobile in your pocket, Ted?'

'Probably.' He ignored it. The beeping stopped.

'Do you fancy stopping on?'

'Hmm?'

'Doing this permanently?'

'What? This?' She stopped and turned to him. 'What are you on about, Ted?'

'The job. Do you want to stop on with us? Permanent, like?'

'Well . . .' She was stunned. 'Are you serious?'

'Why aye! Of course I am. Haven't I just been telling you all the ins and outs?'

She smiled and shook her head with

astonishment. 'I'd love to stay with you! Of course I would. I've enjoyed working here. I'm surprised to hear myself say that, in a way, but I have. It would be wonderful to carry on. Thank you, Ted!'

'That's settled, then. We'll pay you a proper wage, as well, and you'll get the usual benefits. Holidays and such. No more of this minimum wage nonsense.'

She sat down for a moment after Ted had left, coming to terms with what had just happened. It had come so unexpectedly. But she knew one thing. She was pleased. She really was. She wanted the job. She liked it.

Greg, the foreman, came in a few minutes later. 'Congratulations!' he said, wearing a broad smile, an expression she hadn't seen on him before.

She laughed. 'You know? Already?'

He nodded. 'I told you, didn't I?'

'Told me what?'

'Ted keeps good workers on.'

'You did, yes.' She chuckled and shook her head. 'Is that what I am, do you think? A good worker?'

'From the first day,' Greg said. 'All the lads think so.'

Then he gave her a wink and left.

FUTURE PLANS

Things were so much easier and simpler in the weeks and months that followed. Busier too, of course, but Sarah didn't mind that. She never had minded being busy. So she went to work, and afterwards she saw as much as she possibly could of Robert and the children.

They did things together, and it was wonderful. Not big things or exciting once-in-a-lifetime things, just ordinary, everyday things. Like playing football and going for ice-cream. But they did them together, and that made the difference. Made them special.

The way she felt, her whole life had become special.

Linda noticed the change. 'I never see you these days,' she said, catching Sarah emerging from the flat one morning.

'Busy, busy, busy!' Sarah said. 'Having a job to go to makes a difference. I have no spare time.'

'It's not only the job, though, is it?'

'No, it isn't.' Sarah smiled.

'You're going out with someone?'

'Yes. I am.'

'Seriously?'

'Oh, I don't know about that,' she said with a smile.

'But it's fun?'

128

'More than that, Linda. It's . . . everything I've always wanted, really?'

'Good for you! So I was wrong about you and John, wasn't I?'

Sarah nodded and glanced at her watch. 'Sorry. I must fly.'

She walked quickly to work, but not so quickly that she couldn't think about Linda's comment. Yes, Linda had been wrong about her and John. Since that first evening when Robert had taken her out she had known that.

John had not been the one. And Robert was? Oh, she didn't know about that! Far too soon, but he might be. She could dare to hope.

*   *   *

That evening she went straight from work to Robert's house. Robert was going to be late home and she had said she would relieve the child minder for him.

'There you are, Sarah!' Holly cried with delight. 'I was just wondering when you were coming.'

'I'm not late, am I?' she asked, looking at the woman who had been looking after the children.

'No, of course not,' the woman said.

'But I was still wondering where you were,' Holly said. 'I was waiting for you.'

'Well, here I am. What do you want me to do?'

Holly screwed her face up and had a quick think. 'Make me a jam sandwich, and then read me a story, please.'

All right. I can do that. Let me get my coat off first.'

Holly charged off to the kitchen. Sarah smiled at the childminder. 'I assume they've had their tea?'

'Oh, yes.' The woman smiled. 'Holly just wants some attention, that's all.'

'Well, what are we here for?' Sarah said with a smile of her own. 'Where's Jack?'

'Upstairs. He's got one of those computer games.'

'So he's happy for a while?'

'For a little while,' the woman said as she prepared to depart. 'No doubt he'll be hungry again soon, as well.'

'And wanting some attention?'

'That, too!'

*   *   *

Sarah was happy to spend time with the children. She was getting to know them so well, and she could tell they liked her as much as she liked them. Especially Holly.

Robert had said the little girl had missed her mother a lot, perhaps more than Jack had, and it was easy to see that was probably true. When Sarah was there, Holly rarely let her out of sight and was always looking for cuddles.

She was a lovely, affectionate little thing.

That particular evening Sarah read her a story about a princess who lived on a star and travelled by moonbeam or, in good weather, by sunbeam. Holly seemed to find that a perfectly acceptable way to live. She listened with rapt attention until her eyelids failed her and she slumped into a corner of the sofa.

Robert smiled when Sarah told him, and said, 'She's just happy to have you near her. You could tell her anything and she'd listen!'

It was probably true, Sarah decided.

Jack was different. He was older, and he was a boy. He was more emotionally detached, less dependent, and less vulnerable. But he was still glad to have Sarah around. Sarah knew that, and enjoyed the sense of being welcome and wanted.

'Do you want to play chess again?' he asked her that evening.

'Later, Jack. I will later after I've finished this story and got Holly ready for bed.'

'I'm not going to bed tonight,' Holly said, stirring herself. 'I'm staying up with you.'

'Oh? Well, perhaps till Daddy comes home.'

'Yes,' Holly said. 'Till Daddy comes home.' But there was a yawn soon afterwards and Sarah knew the little girl wouldn't last much longer.

She didn't, but Jack did, and he beat her at chess—again!

'You're very good, Jack.'

'Not really. Pete Jenkins is better than me.'

'But you're good, too.'

He shrugged in that false modest way that was so charming. She smiled. She knew that he knew he was good, even if he did know someone who was better.

'Are they in bed?' Robert asked when he came through the door not long after.

'Just. Jack's on his way upstairs. Holly's flat out, though.'

'Well done!' Robert smiled. 'Thanks. How are you?'

'Tired, but I'm fine, Robert. Really.'

He nodded, as if he knew that.

'Are you hungry?' she asked.

'No. I had something. You?'

'I'm OK, too.'

'Oh, well. In that case . . .'

She smiled as he came to her, took her in his arms, gently squeezed her, and kissed her.

'I've been waiting all day for that,' she breathed as he let her go.

He smiled. 'These are good days, aren't they?'

She nodded. 'The best.'

'One of these days,' he said quietly, still holding her, 'we should talk about . . .'

She knew and could guess what was coming. Part of her even wanted to hear it. But . . .

'Ssh!' she said dreamily. 'Not yet.'

They were good days, too. The best of days she had known for such a long time, if not for ever. It was so good to be with Robert. When they were apart, she could hardly stand the wait until she saw him again.

The children, too. She enjoyed being with them all, and the sense of being wrapped up in their warmth. It was wonderful.

Yet . . . and yet . . . she didn't know. Was this where she should be? With Robert? Was this for keeps?

Was it worth dropping her guard and joining with him and the children properly? She knew that was what Robert wanted. The children, too, almost certainly. Yes? Sometimes, most of the time, in fact, she thought yes.

Yet how terrible it would be if, after a while, she found this wasn't where she really wanted to be or that she had outstayed her welcome and they no longer wanted her.

Better, perhaps, to keep Robert and his children—and they were his, the children, after all—at arms' length. Then if the worst happened, it would be easier to weather, the damage limited. Less pain. Less disruption. She had been there once before, and she didn't want to go there again.

'WHAT ABOUT THE CHILDREN?'

'You and Robert seem to be doing very well,' India said.

'Yes. We are.'

'I'm so happy for you—and for Robert.' Sarah smiled.

'This shop, India, is just amazing. I can't believe how absolutely gorgeous you've made it.'

'Don't change the subject!'

'I'm not!'

'You are.'

'Well, I'm very happy. There! That what you want to know?'

'Sit down, Sarah. Just sit down! Have a cup of coffee with me.'

'I'd love to. You know I would. But I'm on my way to the dentist's, that's why I've got the morning off. I just called in to see you for a couple of minutes.'

'Time for a quick cup of coffee,' India said firmly, reaching for the kettle. 'Have you seen these mugs? James Anderson up in Norham makes them.'

Sarah leaned down to study the intricate wildflower pattern. 'They're lovely, aren't they? Where's that?'

'Where's what?'

'Norham.'

'Near Berwick. Inland from Berwick. So what's the problem?'

'Problem?'

'You can't fool me, Sarah. I know something isn't right. What is it? Having second thoughts about Robert?'

134

Sarah sighed and slumped into a chair. 'Oh, I don't know, India. I really don't. In one sense, everything is wonderful. I love Robert and the children. We have such lovely times together. Such normal, ordinary things we do. And I like my job. I like everything about my life now.'

'But?'

Sarah looked up and smiled ruefully.

'There's always a "but", Sarah. We both know that. All sensible people do.'

Sarah chuckled. 'Sensible, India? Is that what we are, you and I?'

'Well, I may not be amazingly sensible sometimes, but you are.'

'Maybe that's the trouble. Do you think it might be?'

'Being too sensible? It easily might.'

Sarah took hold of the coffee cup India passed to her and studied it. Strange how not all the coffee was dissolved. Little bits floated on the surface, like flotsam and jetsam. Like herself, perhaps.

'Sarah!'

She looked up.

'Avoidance therapy doesn't work. I know, I've tried it. I've tried everything in my time.'

Sarah smiled ruefully. 'Oh, you're right, India. There is a "but".'

'What is it this time?'

'Well, what if after a few more months Robert decides he's doesn't have such strong feelings for me, or I for him? It's happened to me before.'

'Is that what you're worried about?'

'What about the children? If Robert and I were to split up later on, how would they feel? I mean, after everything that's already happened in their young lives.'

Sarah stared bleakly at her friend. 'What then?' she said insistently. 'How terrible would it be for us all?'

India sighed. 'There are no guarantees in life, Sarah. You could step in front of a bus tomorrow. Robert could crash that stupid car of his. What about me and Harry? Anything could happen to us—or to anyone else!'

'I know, but . . .'

'But you've been there before,' India said gently. 'That's it, isn't it? You and Marty. You were totally committed, and when it went wrong you found it hard to cope. That's it, isn't it?'

Feeling miserable, Sarah nodded.

'But you did cope. Remember? You moved and started a new life, and now look at you! You did it, Sarah. You proved you can cope.'

'But this time there are children involved— and they're not even mine.'

'Ah! Is that what's bothering you?'

Reluctantly, Sarah nodded. 'A bit, I think. That poor woman . . . It's a big thing, taking over someone else's husband and children. I don't know if I'm strong enough.'

136

'Listen to me. Jenny was a fine person. I knew her well, and I can say this with utter certainty. She was my best friend. Believe me, if Jenny had any say in this, I know what it would be. She would want Robert and the children to be happy. And I know she would like you and want them to be with you. You have no need to worry on that score.'

'Really?'

'Really. More coffee?'

'I'd better not.'

Sarah sighed and stood up. 'You're such a good friend to me, India. And I do trust you. In fact,' she added, 'I've changed my mind about you.'

'In what way?'

'I think you might be a sensible person, after all.'

'Get out of here!'

*   *   *

The dentist let her off lightly. One small filling, and that was it. She was grateful. Added to what India had said, she was feeling a bit better by the time she left the surgery.

Then her mobile rang.

A PANIC ENSUES

It was Robert. 'Holly's missing,' he said quickly with clear panic in his voice.

'What?'

'We can't find her anywhere.'

He was obviously distraught. Sarah tried to stay calm. 'Where have you looked, Robert?'

'The house, the garden, the street. Everywhere! The neighbours haven't seen her. The little girl she plays with. Jack can't find her. I'll have to call the police!'

His voice broke for a moment.

'Hold on, Robert! Just a moment. When did you last see her?'

'A couple of hours ago. It's my fault. Why didn't I . . .'

'What happened, Robert?'

'She was climbing about on the window ledge in her bedroom. I was in the garden. The window was open. I looked up and I ran inside, grabbed her. I told her off. I shouldn't have . . .'

'No, Robert. Of course you should. You did exactly the right thing. It's not your fault, you mustn't think that.'

She thought quickly. In a way, what Robert had said made it seem better. Less likely to be an abduction. Holly told off would not be a happy little girl.

Where would she go? If she was in a strop, what would she do? Hide, probably. Hide and sulk, or hide and rage.

'She'll not be far, Robert. Look, I'm out of the dentist's now and I'm nearly at the garage. I'll just pop in and tell Ted what's going on then I'll come straight over. Don't do anything until I get there.'

She felt Robert was calming down now She could sense it in his voice. The panic was receding. He would behave rationally. Do nothing silly. She was sure of it.

'Hurry,' he said. 'If you can, please hurry.'

She switched off the phone and walked as fast as she could, wishing she had brought the car today. She couldn't get there fast enough First the garage. Then Robert. Nothing could have happened to Holly surely? No, of course not. She wouldn't let it!

She closed off all negative thoughts and concentrated entirely on what she had to do. First see Ted, then see if she could borrow a car to save what might be vital moments.

After that . . . she took a deep breath. After that, do what needed to be done.

Ted was standing in the doorway, looking as if he wished he hadn't stopped smoking his pipe. He smiled as she hurried across the yard.

'I'm glad you've turned up,' he said. 'You've got a visitor. I was just wondering what to do.'

'I can't stop now, Ted. I'm sorry but there's an emergency at Robert's. You'll have to . . .

Who is it?'

He shrugged and stood aside, and ushered her through the doorway.

She stepped into the office and couldn't believe her eyes.

'Holly! What are you doing here? Everyone's looking . . .'

She stopped. No need to frighten her. Holly looked perfectly normal, and was smiling happily.

She rushed over to wrap her arms around the little girl.

'Holly, what are you doing here, darling?'

'I came to see you, Sarah. Daddy was mean to me. He shouted. So I . . .'

'No, he wasn't mean to you. You were doing something very dangerous and he was frightened you would fall out of the window. But how ever did you get here?'

'I just walked.' Holly smiled and kissed her cheek. 'I walked and walked, and I found you, didn't I?'

'Yes, sweetheart. You did.' Sarah closed her eyes for a moment. 'And I'm so glad you did, but you mustn't do that again. Please promise you won't do that again. We were all worried about you.'

'OK,' Holly said with a yawn, danger and other people's fears dismissed, but ready to please someone she loved, and who she knew loved her.

'Her daddy is looking for her,' Sarah said,

turning to Ted. 'I have to go.'

He smiled and nodded. 'Best get her home then. Take my car. Here're the keys.'

'Thanks, Ted. I'll tell you more later.'

'Don't worry about it,' he said. 'I'm glad you've found her—or she's found you! Amazing what little ones can do when they set their mind to it, isn't it?'

Sarah closed her eyes and exhaled with relief. 'You're telling me!'

Holly got to her feet and took firm hold of Sarah's hand.

'Cheerio, Holly!' Ted said with a chuckle.

'Bye, Ted! Thank you for the chocolate.'

'He's a very nice man,' Holly said as Sarah led her out to the car.

'Yes, he is. You're right.'

Sarah carried Holly up the path and into the house.

'Robert!' she called. 'Come and see what I've found.'

With Holly safely in bed, knowing very little of the stir she had caused, Robert pulled Sarah to him. 'Thank you,' he breathed, holding her tight.

'No need,' she said. 'I didn't do much.'

'Yes, you did. You were there for us—for Holly and for me, and Jack as well—when we needed you. You held things together, as you always do.'

'Oh, Robert!'

But she was moved by his words, and by his

obvious feelings for her. She hugged him hard. 'You silly man!' she said. 'I do love you. You know that, don't you?'

He nodded. 'But not as much as I love you.'

Then a little of what India had said came back to her, seeming more powerful and urgent than ever.

'What?' he said, sensing her stiffen.

'Oh, it's just something India said.'

'And what was that?'

'She said we none of us know what's going to happen to us, and it's a good thing we don't.

'Best just to live our lives and not worry about the possibility of problems in the future. If they happen, they happen. And we deal with them. That's it. You can't live in fear of the future.'

'India said all that?'

'Well, not all of it. I made some of it up, but it's what she meant. I've just realised that, and she's right.'

'So?' Robert said, looking puzzled.

'So it means that I want to live my life with you and the children, Robert. Today's little drama has convinced me of that. This is where I belong now—if you'll have me?'

'Now she tells me,' Robert murmured. 'At last!'

'Is that a yes?'

He laughed. And then he kissed her, kissed her like she'd never been kissed before.